All

That Is Left

Is All

That Matters

All

That Is Left

Is All

That Matters

Stories

Mark Slouka

W. W. Norton & Company
Independent Publishers Since 1923
NEW YORK   LONDON

All That Is Left Is All That Matters is a work of fiction. Names, characters, places, and incidents are the products of the author's imagination or are used fictitiously. Any resemblance to actual events, locales, or persons, living or dead, is entirely coincidental.

For information about permission to reproduce selections from this book, write to Permissions, W. W. Norton & Company, Inc., 500 Fifth Avenue, New York, NY 10110

For information about special discounts for bulk purchases, please contact W. W. Norton Special Sales at specialsales@wwnorton.com or 800-233-4830

Manufacturing by Quad Graphics Fairfield
Book design by Fearn Cutler de Vicq
Production manager: Lauren Abbate

Library of Congress Cataloging-in-Publication Data
Names: Slouka, Mark, author.
Title: All that is left is all that matters : stories / Mark Slouka.
Description: First edition. | New York : W. W. Norton & Company, 2018.
Identifiers: LCCN 2017060266 | ISBN 9780393292282 (hardcover)
Subjects: LCSH: Life change events—Fiction. |
Control (Psychology)—Fiction. | Psychological fiction.
Classification: LCC PS3569.L697 A6 2018 | DDC 813/.54—dc23
LC record available at https://lccn.loc.gov/2017060266

W. W. Norton & Company, Inc.
500 Fifth Avenue, New York, N.Y. 10110
www.wwnorton.com

W. W. Norton & Company Ltd.
15 Carlisle Street, London W1D 3BS

1 2 3 4 5 6 7 8 9 0

For Leslie, Maya, and Zack,
who will always be home,
wherever the world may find me.

And he wondered whether death might not be
vulnerable to an invasion of his own territory.

—W. G. SEBALD

Contents

All

That Is Left

Is All

That Matters

Dominion

THEY'D ALWAYS SLEPT WITH THE WINDOWS OPEN. Even now, late into the season, with the husks of the cicadas dangling like Chinese lanterns in the webs below the eaves, they'd swing the frames up to the ceiling, mating hook to eye: one toward the dirt road, another toward the upsloping woods, two toward the old pasture wall that ran straight into the lake and disappeared like a man determined to drown himself. Not that you could see any of these things—on moonless nights, opening the windows was like punching holes into a barrel—but they were there. They always had been.

He didn't know where the coyotes had come from, or how long they'd been there. A season, maybe two. The dairy farms were falling fast, replaced by things named after whatever had been destroyed to make room for them, but there were still enough woods left to allow for a pack or two. Now, with the leaves almost down, you could hear them all the way out toward the state park. It always started the same way: a series of quick, laughing yips that pulled you out of your sleep, three, four, five voices, almost joyful, falling over one another like pups until one would suddenly catch and hold, as though impaled, mid-laugh, and then the others would follow, stricken in turn, rising, barking, screaming, a braided chorus of hilarity and pain. These were not dogs.

He didn't know what it was. He'd awoken the first time in a well of fear, unable to breathe.

"Hear that?" he'd whispered into the dark, needing to wake her.

"What on earth . . . ?"

Her voice was sanity, bottom, ground. The world corrected itself. "What am I listening to?" she asked.

"I think they're coyotes," he said, slipping back inside himself, resuming his place.

"Since when do we have coyotes?" she whispered back.

HE HADN'T KNOWN what he was listening to at first, what it was he was hearing—hadn't been able to place it at all. He'd been dreaming something . . . bad, and for a few moments it had been as though the dream, the madness of it, had followed him out into the waking world, clinging to him like a piece of tape stuck to the middle of his back.

They lay side by side, listening. At the base of the wall of voices he could now make out a simple screaming—something being killed.

"Good God," she said.

"Sounds like they got something," he said. The screams changed into a high, repetitive keening, like a broken mechanism.

"We have to do something," she said.

"Like what?"

"Make a noise or something."

"They're a quarter of a mile away."

Outside in the blackness something was choking wetly. It was oddly embarrassing to listen to it. He had to say something, cover this.

"I saw in the paper they found one in Central Park," he said, and that instant saw a small, blue motel room sixty years ago, the two of them trying to talk over the cries and grunts coming from the landscape hanging over the bed as their daughter colored in a picture on a round table—"Said it had to have walked over one of the bridges during the night."

"Into Manhattan?"

"That's where they keep Central Park."

"I don't believe it. Sounds like alligators in the sewers to me."

"Said they're cunning little bastards. Tough as a shovel. That they'll go anywhere."

"Did it say where they came from?"

"Didn't say. I think . . ."

They were going, dropping quickly into silence. The quiet spread: thick, cool paint on glass.

"I think it's over," she said.

"I think it is," he said.

He could feel himself beginning to unclench. He wished he could remember now what the article had said—whether they had come out of the west, spreading east through the plains and the cornfields as the predators died before them, or whether they had always been there, right from the beginning, and only been squeezed into visibility by the loss of their space. He seemed to recall that both theories had their backers. It hardly mattered. Domestic or imported, they were here.

"I've never heard anything like that before in my life," she said, turning over on her side.

They hunted like cats, he remembered now, stalking and leaping on the backs of their prey rather than running it down like wolves.

HE LAY AWAKE for an hour after that, listening, waiting for them to return, trying to understand what had happened to him. In the first few moments, as he'd plunged from sleep like a swimmer rushing from the water, he'd distinctly imagined a giant muzzle crashing through the roof of the cabin, snuffing and snatching at flesh as though they were voles in a burrow. The madness of that image, so uncharacteristic of him, troubled him now. He had never been particularly bothered by the ferocity of nature before, had always known, and accepted the fact, that the border between life and death was a porous thing, the two sides bleeding into each other everywhere and always. And yet, though he understood all this and more, having served in France at a time when the borders had been fixed and hard and the bleeding pretty much all one way, there was something else going on here.

SOMETIMES, LATELY, HE'D wake up in the middle of the night and lean over her to see if she was breathing. Twice in the last year, unable to hear anything, he'd shaken her awake, fighting off the panic tightening his chest and rising into his throat like glue. "What's wrong? What is it?" she'd cried out both times, bolting up into the dark, and both times he'd had to invent some absurd story, once that he'd had a nightmare, the other, more shamefully, that he had no idea what she was talking about, that she was the one who had woken him. "What? What is it?" he'd begun yelling the instant she sprang awake, making a big show of being disoriented and confused. When she asked him what this was all about, and whether he had finally lost his mind, waking her up in the middle of the night, he'd allowed himself to get angry. "Why the hell would I want to wake you?" he'd demanded, and spent the next few minutes arguing so convincingly, so self-righteously, that by the time he'd rolled over on his other side he half believed that it was she who had woken him, and resented her for it.

At night he would lie looking up into the cedar planks or out through the open windows into the dark, weighing his life, adding a little dust here, a little there, shaking it in his palm, then raining it out like salt. The scales tipped and creaked.

ARTHUR PROCHASKA HAD been a journalist with the *Hartford Courant* for fifty-nine years. He'd think about that sometimes. He'd started there when he was sixteen, two years after armistice, less than three after his father died—a tough, ringwormy-looking kid in borrowed shoes who did whatever was asked of him. The old guys, who didn't like anybody, had taken a shine to him right off. It had all been an accident, the way it had turned out. A noisy argument had broken out around O'Connor's desk, where the boys had gathered, as usual, to shoot the shit and pass judgment on whoever seemed in need of it. God how he'd loved the place.

"Hell, any kid off the street could tell you that," he heard someone say as he walked into the mailroom.

"Hey, you," O'Connor had called out to him—"Yeah, you. What's your name?" Arthur told him. O'Connor waved it away. "Jesus, all right, get over here. You can read, right?" He snapped a sheet of paper at him. "Read this."

And seventeen-year-old Artie Pro-kaska, who hadn't even gotten laid yet though he'd thought about it a good deal, who didn't know shit from shinola, who had nothing but a pair of oversized shoes and a bit of moxie with which to front the world, opened his mouth and a legend flew out—a miracle of deadpan delivery and Swiss-watch timing. Everyone was there: Franks, with his leg up over the corner of the desk; Maroni, looking like the bagged-out welterweight he was; old Ralph Simmes, forever rolling a spit-black inch of stogie between his teeth—all of them, including himself, blissfully unaware that they were calcifying into newsroom clichés, becoming in some basic way unbelievable. "Well?" O'Connor had growled after some seconds had passed. "Not too bad," the kid pronounced, still looking at the paper. "What's his first language?"

And there it was. Just like that. Afterward, all he'd have to do was not smile or, when he did, make it look like it hurt. The old guard protected him, laughed at his mistakes, created openings: "Give it to the kid. What about the kid? Let the kid take a whack at it." Maroni, seeing him reading something, would call: "Hey, kid, what do you think—French?" and all he would have to do was not look up but stare at the paper a moment, considering it—"Well . . ." and it was in the bag. His line, which owed everything to the gods of chance, who could turn the world on its head in an instant, became as much a part of the atmosphere as the ring-and-smack of the carriage returns. One generation passed it on to the next like a well-fingered baton.

A blessed life, in many ways. He'd enjoyed the newsroom, resisted all attempts to move him up and away from it. He'd loved everything about it: the smell—like smoke and sweat and something very much like the inside of a brass pot; the harsh, industrial lighting; the immovable metal-topped desks . . . loved getting up to go to the cooler just to see the room sit up and tighten, so to speak, the younger men hunching over their typewriters or pulling pencils from behind their ears, the older ones deliberately leaning back in their swivel chairs and leafing through some papers to show that, like him, they didn't need to look busy to get the job done. He liked this generalized awareness of himself, this constant reflecting back. He hadn't realized how much. Once or twice, after he'd left, he'd felt as though he'd disappeared.

Which he had, really. On the day he retired he'd received a plaque, a pen, a bottle of Champagne, and a rectangular black jewelry box in which a row of printer's type, buried up to the pin mark in cotton, spelled out "Thank you, Arthur P." He drank the Champagne, kept the pen, tossed the plaque and the jewelry box in the kitchen garbage. Whose bright idea had *that* been?

And that was that. He was gone, yanked, pulled like a hair. Off the radar. A butterfly flaps its wings, he thought, and not a goddamned thing happens in China. He recognized himself for what he was—a retirement cliché—and ridiculed himself for it, but that didn't make it go away. He still felt thin somehow—transparent. He couldn't help it. Less than a month later, walking through the midday crowd along Main Street, he had been over-come by the sense that he could do anything he wanted—take out his dick and piss in his hat, run out of a store with an arm-ful of brassieres—and no one would notice. No one. Everything around him had grown strangely quiet, the sounds of voices and traffic receding as though they were all on the back of an invisible truck moving steadily away from him. He'd stood there in the hot sun until he became aware of the fact that he was breathing very high and fast, as though his lungs had shrunk to the size of a fist, and then, not knowing what else to do, had sat down on a nearby bench. It passed. The next day he had himself checked out, think-ing it might have been a stroke of some kind, but nothing.

He'd decided not to say anything to Janice. It wasn't that he was worried she'd overreact—she'd always been a practical woman, good at seeing what was there and no more—just that he didn't much care for the picture of himself going on. That was never the way it had been between them—he'd never played the child with her—and he wasn't about to start changing things now.

They'd been married for damn near sixty years. At night when they went to sleep he'd press up against her back and reach around and cup one of her big, soft breasts with his right hand, then move down to her stomach, whose skin was soft and foldy like the fur on those socklike dogs that had been so fashionable a few years back. She would reach behind and give him an affec-tionate squeeze, and though it didn't lead to anything anymore like it used to, that was all right.

God in heaven but how he used to ride her. In this very room, in fact, though the beds had changed over the years, rocked out of joint one after the other, including one that had actually crashed to the floor in the middle of things, scaring the hell out of them both. Janice Vaculik—who would have believed it? Seemed like that first year they couldn't get enough of each other—she was always grabbing at him, sneaking a squeeze even under her parents' dinner table or whispering in his ear, making him hard on the bus—but even after, when the imagination had taken over and they had begun to dare each other further and further into thinking things that shamed and excited them, it had been good. Very good. He still remembered it—the stored up feeling of it, the anticipation of it.

Arthur Prochaska rolled over on his back. The antique scales on his chest, their base nestled down into the mat of hair, rose and fell. The first house, the second, the view from the bedroom window, the faces of the kids . . . They'd done all right. Better than all right. He had no complaints, nor any right to any.

BUT RIGHT HAS no claim in the court of our fears. As Arthur Prochaska was sliding sideways into sleep, the inevitability of his own death suddenly slipped up and seized him by the throat. He struggled and thrashed, knowing it would pass, brought his usual weapons to bear: Everyone had to die. Others died young, or in pain, or alone. He himself could have died a half a century ago in France. He called himself names: He was an ungrateful bastard, a coward, the worst kind of egotist, whining for a special dispensation, unable to imagine the world without him. Sit up, you fool, he said to himself, and sat up in bed in the dark and then, like a man pushing back a great dark wall on rollers, began to think of other things, moving the thing inch by inch from his mind. He got up and walked to the kitchen, his toes curling up from the cold floor, and poured himself a drink. Fuck it. He was fine. When he came back to bed Janice was still sleeping.

It was such a simple thing. You really had to laugh. He was eighty-seven years old, with spots on his temples and odd little tags of skin on his arms and legs and neck, and he didn't want to die. But that wasn't it, exactly. It wasn't so much that he didn't want to die—Who would?—as that he simply couldn't conceive of it. It had been a problem, off and on, for as long as he could remember. How could the moment come when he would no longer be conscious of the world? He understood death. He'd written about it, seen more than his share of it. And yet, when it came right down to it, he didn't understand it at all. How could you be alive, and then not? How could the great doors close forever, sweeping over the sky, the trees . . . ?

He had always thought it was something he'd understand once he got closer to it, like algebra. That his occasional episodes (for that was what he thought of them as) would pass with age. That like a forest, which seems solid from a distance but is actually filled with paths, death would explain itself on closer acquaintance. It hadn't happened that way. And now here he was. Bummer, as the young people said.

IT WASN'T UNTIL he'd seen it go by with the cat that he knew it was death. Lowercase death, unemphatic and certain. It was just after lunch, a strangely warm November afternoon. He was sitting at the too-tall desk by the window, trying to work, when it appeared, a long-legged, unhealthy-looking creature at once arrogant and supplicant, and looked at him—that is, looked at him as he sat there in dreaming disbelief as it trotted straight across the yard and along the wall, then disappeared out of sight into the undergrowth. There had been a hand-sized patch of fur missing on its right flank. A rusty cat was hanging from its jaws.

Janice had been in the other room, reading by the window. "Oh, my God, I just . . ." he started to call out, still half-disbelieving what he'd seen, and then for some reason stopped himself. He heard the chair springs in the other room. "Arthur?"

"Right here," he said. "I swear to God I just had it right here. Not five seconds ago." He heard her settle back in the chair. "You want some more coffee?" she said, and he heard the newspaper. Some days later, when a young couple who lived down the road came by asking whether they had seen their cat, he didn't have the heart or the courage to tell them. It was like a secret he'd pledged to keep. And anyway it was done.

He was fine during the days, reading in the hammock, carrying small bundles of kindling into the cabin, cleaning out the shed. A late fall. When they went for their walks now, the walls that marked the old pastures were visible everywhere, and yet during the afternoons sometimes he would still hear the high trill of crickets that should have been gone long ago. A cold sound, thin and perfect. The lake was tea-black and still. On warm days he could hear the wasps under the eaves and one morning nearly bit into one that was walking carefully along the edge of his toast.

And yet it was always there now, like a shape hidden in a

drawing. He could sense it in the trees and the lichened boulders of the walls, in the late light on the water, in the black rim of shore reflected in the pond. An absurd conceit. During the days it was deniable, laughable. At night it wasn't. He was exhausted now. Every night he'd snap awake and lie there listening, clammy with sweat and self-disgust, unable to escape that ridiculous equation: they were it. It was as though, once imagined, the thing had taken on a life that could not be denied. He didn't know what he was afraid of, exactly, and yet he was afraid. Again and again it trotted through his world, its head turned to the window behind which he sat frozen, and disappeared over the wall. There was the ugly, hand-sized patch of skin on its haunch. It looked at him over the floppy-legged body in its mouth, then leaped the stones, the cat's head swinging back and forth like a child's doll with its stuffing removed. And there it was again. It trotted past the window. There was the ugly patch of hairless skin, the cat's head swinging . . . and again.

It did no good to argue. Once it had taken hold, there was nothing he could do. Getting up didn't help; reading didn't help. He knew they weren't a threat—not literally. And yet it didn't matter. It was as though everything had been turned upside down inside of him, reason itself revealed as a lifelong artifice, a reef of tiny lies and rationalizations. They were coming back. He was going to die. It scared him witless. It broke his heart.

He said nothing. He unscrewed the ladder from the dock, dragged it into the shed, then pushed dirt over the two narrow furrows he'd dug into the grass. The weather had turned. A windless gloom had settled over the water, the stones, the hills. Everything seemed emptied out now, an exercise in perspective:

the three dead trees by the dam, the wooden float. The day had dawned so dark that hearing Janice in the kitchen he thought she had gotten up early. It was almost ten.

By noon it was dusk. He busied himself bringing in more wood, then took a phone call from his son in the city. Everything was fine. At four it started to rain, a thick, soaking rain, and he made a fire. He tried to read but couldn't. He'd always loved a fire on rainy days: the crack and spit of the wood, the sweet, sharp smell. It filled him with sadness now. Once or twice he had a glimpse of himself, trapped in a peculiar box of his own making, but it passed like a scent, like the idlest whimsy, like an offhand remark, and was gone. At nine thirty he went to bed.

HE FELL ASLEEP almost immediately—a deep, drowning sleep. It was night, and something was in the lake. He couldn't reach it. He dragged the heavy ladder back to the water, lowered it down, felt something grasp it in the dark. Somebody was calling his name from the cabin. Just a minute, he called. He had to do this. He struggled to pull the ladder from the water, to save this thing. It was working. He grabbed a lower rung, hauled up with all his strength. Something was wrong—it was coming up too quickly. He grasped another rung, and another. The ladder had never been this long. Even before he saw it, he was struggling to run, unable to unclench his hands from the wet wood: a paleness, a hand-sized circle, rising up to the surface, screaming.

And suddenly he was awake and it was all around him: a continent of sound, shoving in from the dark. It seemed to be everywhere at once, a guttural, howling chorus, just beyond the open window. He couldn't move, he couldn't breathe. There was nothing out there. Nothing but darkness, endless, interminable. My God, he thought: so this is how it is.

Something soft fell across his chest. There was a small, jostling crash, a quick curse, then a rush to the window. A beam like a sword flashed into the darkness, even as an infuriate voice yelled into the void: "Shut up, you stupid mutts!"

Silence, abrupt as a slammed door.

The beam clicked off. He listened to her walk back around to her end of the bed, knowing her body, feeling it negotiating the obstacles as though it were his own. "Goddamnit, I'm going to have this bruise for a week," he heard her say. "When are you going to put some padding on that corner like I keep asking you to?" She climbed back in, turned on her side. "Next time it's your turn," she said.

A great clarity, like cold water, like oxygen. Arthur Prochaska lay on his back. He wanted to laugh. It was gone, cracked like an egg. Boo! he whispered to himself.

He looked around the room. There was the sloping ceiling, the hanging coat, the mirror to the other bedroom in which they lay. There were the four windows, open like mouths. And beyond them? Beyond them was the known world: the lake, the boulders of the wall, the endless, shoreless forest.

The Hare's Mask

ODD HOW I MISS HIS VOICE, AND YET IT'S HIS silences I remember now: the deliberateness with which he moved, the way he'd listen, that particular smile, as if, having long ago given up expecting anything from the world, he continually found himself mugged by its beauty. My father. Even as a kid I wanted to protect him, and because he saw the danger in this, he did what he could.

I didn't make it easy. By the time I was five I'd figured out— the way kids usually do, by putting pieces together and working them until they fit—that he'd lost his parents and sister during the war. That they'd been there one morning, like keys on a table, then gone. When I asked he said it had been so long ago that it seemed like another life, that many bad things had happened then, that these were different times, and then he messed up my hair and smiled and said, "None of us are going anywhere, trust me." But I knew better. When we went to the doctor he'd make funny faces and joke around while the doctor put a needle in his arm to show me it didn't hurt. And it came to me that everything he did—the way he'd turn the page of a book, or laugh with me at *Krazy Kat*, or call us all into the kitchen on Saturday evenings to see the trout he'd caught lying on the counter, their sticky skin flecked with bits of fern—was just the same.

He used to tie his own trout flies, and as a boy I'd come down late at night when we still lived in the old house, sneaking past the yellow bedroom where my sister slept in her crib, stepping over the creaking mines, and he'd be sitting there at the dining-room table with just the one lamp, his hooks and feathers and furs spread out on the wood around him, and when he saw me he'd sit me on his knee, my stockinged feet dangling around his calves, and show me things. "Couldn't sleep?" he'd say. "Look here, I'll show you something important." And he'd catch the bend of a hook in the long-nosed vise and let me pick the color of the thread, and I'd watch him do what he did, his thin, strong fingers winding the waxed strand back from the eye or stripping the webbing off a small feather or clipping a fingernail patch of short, downy fur from the cheek of a hare. He didn't explain and I didn't ask. He'd just work, now and then humming a few notes of whatever he'd been listening to—Debussy or Chopin, Mendelssohn or Satie—and it would appear, step by step, the slim, segmented thorax, the gossamer tail, the tiny, barred wings, and he'd say, "Nice, isn't it?" and then, "Is it done?" and I'd shake my head, because this was how it always went, and he'd say, "OK, now watch," and his fingers would loop and settle the thread and draw it tight so quickly it seemed like one motion, then clip the loose end close to the eye with the surgical scissors. "Some things you can finish," he'd say.

———

I DON'T KNOW how old I was when I was first drawn to their faces on the mantelpiece—not old. When I was alone I'd pull up a chair and stand on it and look at them: my grandfather, tall, slim, stooped, handsome, his thinning hair in full retreat at thirty; my grandmother with her sad black eyes and her uncomfortable smile—almost a wince—somehow the stronger of the two; my aunt, a child of four, half turned toward her mother as if about to say something . . . My father stood to the right, an uncomfortable eight-year-old in a high-necked shirt and tie, a ghost from the future. I'd look at this photograph and imagine him taking it down when we weren't around, trying to understand how it was possible that they could be gone all this time and only him left behind. And from there, for some reason, I'd imagine him remembering himself as a boy. He'd be standing in the back of a train at night, the metal of the railing beneath his palms. Behind him, huddled together under the light as if on a cement raft, he'd see his family, falling away so quickly that already he had to strain to make out their features, his father's hat, his mother's hand against the black coat, his sister's face, small as a fingertip . . . And holding on to the whitewashed mantelpiece, struggling to draw breath into my shrinking lungs, I'd quickly put the picture back as though it were something shameful. Who knows what somber ancestor had passed on to me this talent, this precocious ear for loss? For a while, because of it, I misheard almost everything.

IT BEGAN WITH the hare's mask. One of the trout flies my father tied—one of my favorites because of its name—was the Gold

Ribbed Hare's Ear, which required, for its bristly little body, a tiny thatch of hare's fur, complete with a few long, dark guard hairs for effect. My father would clip the hair from a palm-sized piece of fall-colored fur, impossibly soft. For some reason, though I knew fox was fox and deer hair, deer hair, I never read the hare's mask as the face of a hare, never saw how the irregular outline spoke the missing eyes, the nose . . . Whatever it was—some kind of optical illusion, some kind of mental block—I just didn't see it, until I did.

Which brings me—I've gone ahead of myself a little—to the story of the rabbits. I must have overheard them talking one night when they thought I was sleeping—my parents, that is—and made of it what I could, creeping back up to my room with that new and troubling puzzle piece that I would have to place, and would, in my way. I couldn't have known much.

The full story was this. As a young boy growing up on Táborská Street in Brno, Czechoslovakia, my father would have to go out to the rabbit hutch in the evenings to tend the rabbits and, on Friday nights, kill one for dinner. It was a common enough chore in those days, but he hated doing it. He'd grow attached, give them names, agonize endlessly. Often he'd cry, pulling on their ears, unable to choose one or, having chosen, to hit it with the stick. Sometimes he'd throw up. Half the time he'd make a mess of it anyway, hitting them too low or too high so they'd start to kick and he'd drop them on the floor and have to do it again. Still, this is what boys did, whether they liked it or not, and so he did what was expected of him.

In September of 1942, when he was nine, three months after the partisans assassinated Reichsprotektor Reinhard Heydrich in Prague, my father's family hid a man in the rabbit hutch. My grandfather, who had fought with the Legionnaires in Italy in 1917, built a false wall into the back, making a space two meters long and a half meter wide. There was no light. You couldn't stand up. The man, whose name my father never knew, but who may have been Miloš Werfel who was captured soon afterward and sent to Terezín, where he was killed the following spring, stayed for nine days.

Both had their burdens. My father, who had to go on making his miserable trips to the hutch to keep from attracting the neighbors' attention, now had to slide a food plate through the gap between the false wall and the floorboards, then take the bucket of waste to the compost pile, dump it, clean it out, return it. By the time he was done taking care of the rabbits, the plate would be empty. Werfel, for his part, lying quietly in the dark, broken out in sores, had to endure my father's Hamlet-like performances. To whack, or not to whack. There were bigger things than rabbits.

Nine days. What strange, haunted hours those must have been that they spent in each other's company, neither one able to acknowledge the other (my father was under strict orders, and Werfel knew better), yet all the time aware of the other's presence, hearing the slow shift of cloth against wood or air escaping the nose or even, in Werfel's case, glimpsing some splinter of movement through a crack.

Who knows what Werfel thought? Poet, partisan, journalist, Jew—each an indictment in itself, any combination worthy of death—he must have known where things stood. Not just with himself, but with the boy who brought him food and took the bucket with his waste. Partisans weren't supposed to have children—this was just one of those things. As for my father, he didn't think about Werfel much, if in fact it was Werfel who hid there those nine days. He didn't think how strange it was that a grown man, his suit carefully folded in a rucksack, should be lying in his underwear behind a board in the rabbit hutch. He didn't think about what this meant, or what it could mean. He thought about Jenda and Elíška.

Jenda and Elíška were rabbits, and they were a problem. That September, for whatever reason, my father's uncle Lada hadn't been able to bring the family any rabbits, and the hutch was almost empty. Jenda and Elíška were the last. My father, who had been protecting the two of them for months by taking others in their place, thought about little else. With that unerring masochism common to all imaginative children, he'd made them his own. They smelled like fur and alfalfa. They trusted him. Whenever he came in, they'd hop over to him and stand up like rabbits in a fairy tale, hooking their little thick-clawed feet on the wire. They couldn't live without each other. It was impossible. What he had yet to learn is that the impossible is everywhere; that it hems us in at every turn, trigger set, ready to turn when touched.

And so it was. Locked in by habit, my father had to go to the hutch to keep Mrs. Čermaková from asking after his health because the other evening she'd just happened to notice my grandfather going instead, had to go because habit was safety, invisibility, because it held things together, or seemed to, even as they were falling apart; because even in this time of routine outrages against every code and norm—*particularly* in this time—the norm demanded its due. And so off he went, after the inevitable scene, the whispering, the tears, shuffling down the dirt path under the orchard, emerging ten minutes later holding the rabbit in his arms instead of by its feet, disconsolate, weeping, schooled in self-hatred . . . but invisible. The neighbors were used to his antics.

It wasn't enough, something had been tripped; the impossible opened like a bloom. Two days after my father, his eyes blurring and stinging, brought the stick down on the rabbit's back, the hutch felt different; Werfel was gone. Five days later, just before nine o'clock on the morning of October 16, 1942, my father's parents and sister were taken away. My father never saw them again. He himself, helping out in a neighbor's garden at the time, escaped. It shouldn't have been possible.

And the train, obscenely, magnificently, pulled on. Sixteen years later my father had emigrated to New York, married a woman he met at a dance hall who didn't dance, and moved into an apartment on Sixty-Third Road in Queens, a block down from the Waldbaum's. Four years after that, having traded proximity to Waldbaum's for an old house in rural Putnam County, he'd acquired a son, a daughter, and the unlikely hobby of trout fishing. And in 1969, that daughter came to the table, poured some milk on her Cap'n Crunch, and announced that she wanted a rabbit for her sixth birthday.

WHICH IS WHERE I come in. I'd begun to understand some things by this time, to work some things out—I was almost nine. I knew, though he'd never show it, how hard this business with the rabbit would be for him, how much it would remind him of. Though I couldn't say anything in front of him, I did what I could behind the scenes. I offered my sister my gerbils, sang the virtues of guinea pigs, even offered to do her chores. When she dug in, predictably—soon enough it was a rabbit or death—I called her stupid, and when she started to cry, then hit me in the face with a plastic doll, I tried to use that to get the rabbit revoked. It didn't work. She'd been a good girl, my mother said, incredibly. We lived in the country. I had gerbils. It wasn't unreasonable.

That weekend we drove to the pet store in Danbury (I could come too if I behaved myself, my mother said), and after a last attempt to distract us from our mission by showing my sister the hamsters running on their wheels or pawing madly at the glass, I watched as my father leaned over the pen, lifting out one rabbit after the other, getting pine shavings on his lap while she petted their twitching backs or pulled their stupid ears . . . I wanted to hit her. When I took my father's hand at one point he looked down at me and said, "You OK?" and I said, "Sure." My sister picked out an ugly gray one with long ears, and as we were leaving the store I stuck out my foot and she hit herself on one of the metal shelves and my father grabbed me and said, "What's the matter with you, what's gotten into you these days?" and I started to cry.

It got worse. I wouldn't help set it up. I wouldn't feed it. I refused to call it by its name. I started calling it Blank for some reason. When my sister asked me something about it, I'd say "Who? You mean Blank?" and when she started to cry I'd feel bad but I couldn't stop and part of me felt better. When it kept my sister up at night with its thumping and rustling, and my parents moved its cage to the living room, I started walking around the other way, through the kitchen. I'd pretend to myself that I couldn't look at it, that something bad would happen if I did, and even watching TV I'd put my hand up as if scratching my forehead, or thinking, so that my eye couldn't slip. Sometimes I'd catch my dad looking at me, and once he asked me if I'd like a rabbit of my own. When I said no, he pretended to be surprised, and for some reason I wanted to cry.

It was sometime that fall that I had a bad dream and came down the stairs to find him sitting at the table under the lamp, tying his trout flies. He looked up at me over the silly half-glasses that went over his regular glasses that helped him to see. "Well, hello," he said. "Haven't done this in a while."

"I couldn't sleep," I said.

"Bad dream?"

"No," I said. I could hear the rabbit in the dark behind us, thumping around in his cage.

"He can't sleep either," my father said.

"What's that one called?" I said, pointing to the fly he had in the vise.

My dad was looking at me. "This one?" he said. And he told me, then showed me how it was made, clipping four or five blue-gray spears for the tail, then selecting a single strand from a peacock feather for the body. I watched him secure it with a few loops of thread, then start to wind it toward the eye of the hook, the short dark hairs sparking green with every turn through the light . . . And that's when I saw it, not just the thick, familiar, chestnut fur of the cheeks and head and neck, but now, for the first time, the missing nose and ears, the symmetrical cavities of the eyes, even the name itself, reaching back to deepest child- hood through the medium of my father's voice saying, "Pass me the hare's mask," "Let's take a little bit off the hare's mask," all of it revealed at last, and in that moment knew, in my dim way, that he'd been enduring the long needle of association, of memory, for years. He was never free of it.

It was the next day that I took the hare's mask and hid it in my room. When he asked me if I'd seen it I lied, and when he came back upstairs after going through everything in the dining room (as though that piece of fur could have jumped from the table and hidden itself behind his books) I swore I didn't have it and even let myself get indignant over the fact that he wouldn't believe me. Eventually he left. "For Christ's sake," I heard him saying to my mother downstairs, "it didn't just disappear," and then, "That's not the point and you know it."

I slept with it under my pillow. I'd keep it in my pocket and run my thumb over the thin edge of the eye socket and the soft bristly parts where my father had clipped it short. When no one was home I'd hold it up to the rabbit cage and, appalled at myself, thrilled and shaky, yell "Look, look, this was you" to the rabbit, who would sometimes hop over and try to nibble at it through the wires. I pushed my nose into it, breathing in that indescrib- able deep fur smell.

And that's how he found me, holding the hare's mask against my face, crying so hard I didn't hear him come into the room. Two days before my ninth birthday. Because he'd understood about dates, and how things that aren't connected can seem to be, and that he'd been nine years old when it happened. And he held me for a long time, petting my hair in that slightly awkward, fatherly way, saying "It's OK, everything's going to be OK, everything's just fine." Which it was.

It was some years later that I asked him and he told me how it went that night. How he'd opened the dirt-scraping door to the hutch and entered that too-familiar smell of alfalfa and steel and shit already sick with the knowledge that he couldn't do what he absolutely had to do. How he lit the lamp and watched them hop over to him. How he stood there by the crate, sobbing, pulling first on Jenda's ears, then Elíška's, picking up one, then the other, pushing his nose into their fur, telling them how much he loved them . . . unaware of the time passing, unaware of anything, really—this is how miserable he is—until suddenly a man's voice speaks from behind the wall and says, "You're a good boy. Let me choose." My father laughed—a strange laugh: "And I remember standing there with my hands in the wire and feeling this stillness come over me, and him saying, 'Jenda. Take Jenda, he's the weaker of the two. It's not wrong. Do it quickly.'"

Then

I COULDN'T TELL YOU WHAT SENT ME INTO THE city that day. A gathering of things. Of sadness, maybe. It's always been that way, like I'd been born to swing between sun and shade. I've made peace with it—or tried. A professor at Columbia (I can still see his little marsupial face, that polka-dot bow tie) would look at me over his half-glasses when I came to his office and ask: "Well, and what are we today, Mr. Panakoupolis, imbued or embalmed?"

So I guess you could say that I went into town because I'd felt myself swinging toward the embalmed side of things. Ordinary thoughts, dreams, but no less painful for not being original. About my father, wrapping up and not inclined to go gently, about time, about mortality, the speed of things . . .

My problem is that like Sir Gawain I love my life too much, and loving anything too much, as the Green Knight explained—particularly ourselves—breeds cowardice. I've had moments when I've been almost paralyzed by fear, mute, a rabbit in the crosshairs—but I've also had times when the world began to speak, when everything—the drops in the screen, the smell of cedar drying in the sun, the laughter of kids cracking each other up on the subway—burst into song and I knew, I *knew*, with absolute, laughing certainty, that death was nothing—a chuckle, a quip, a long stretch and a wink—when I felt, well, imbued.

My father had written to say that what annoyed him most about the whole business of dying was that you couldn't, as the saying goes, take it with you—not a single goddamn thing—that it would make it so much easier if it was like it used to be before a camping trip when he could just lay out his stuff on the Ping-Pong table and decide what to bring. He'd take a picture of me if he could figure out how, he said, and the elf that's sat on his windowsill for eighteen years ever since our daughter gave it to him, its pipe-cleaner legs dangling over the glass. A couple of other things. A small duffel would do it, he said.

I wrote back and told him not to worry about packing because the bag would just sit around getting in the way, unless of course he wanted to speed things up, in which case he could leave it on the top of the stairs in the dark. The usual bravado and bullshit—as good a way of dealing with the things you can't deal with as any.

So I went into town. I don't think I showed it, but Kate could tell: "Go, for God's sake. Have lunch with Mac, it'll do you good. Have a drink. Have two." I argued—I was fine—but in the end I trudged down the hill and got on the Metro-North and sat by the window like a cloud in a coat staring out at the half-frozen reservoirs and the garbage that shows up every year just in time for Thanksgiving, and things just got uglier until by Yonkers the box springs and the refrigerators and the baby carriages scrolling across the window were chanting it in unison, just for me: "It flies, it flies, you too shall die."

MAC AND I SPENT lunch talking about his knees, which didn't improve things. He'd been a scared eighteen-year-old from Santo Domingo when he walked into our dormitory room: wiry, balanced, quick as a ferret on the soccer pitch. Now he was running the emergency room at Mt. Sinai on bum knees. He was going to get them replaced—an upgrade.

"A year from now I'll kick your skinny white ass just like I used to," he said.

I told him his memory needed an upgrade too.

No incentive, he said. Who the hell wanted a good memory? He checked his watch. He had the car—could he drop me somewhere?

I'd walk, I said. It was a nice day, and I still had the knees for it.

I WAS HEADING DOWN to Riverside, choosing the promenade of Jamaican nannies over the wall of banks that used to be Broadway, when I saw her—or someone who looked like her—and as we passed we glanced up, then looked again, then pivoted like disbelieving bullfighters and stopped. "Jesus Christ," she said, and touched my cheek: "What on earth happened to your hair?"

"Left," I said, "didn't leave a note."

For just a second I could see her as she'd been—that self-assured mouth, the easy way she moved, as if her body were an open coat she'd thrown on at the last instant—and then she was gone.

"You look good, Allie," I said.

"Liar." That smile—amusement and tenderness—hadn't changed much. She was still looking at me: "Jesus Christ," she whispered.

"I assure you, no," I said.

SO WE FOUND a diner, a booth by the window, and the whole time I just kept thinking how very strange it was for the two of us to be sitting there taking turns reading off the lists of people we'd loved, the things we'd done, the places we'd lived while all the time wanting to shout, "Hold on, stop! How the hell did *this* happen? How did you go out for cigarettes while I picked the clothes off the floor and come back like this? And how on earth did I get to be sixty-fucking-four?

But honesty and cruelty are joined at the lip, as my mother liked to say, so I let it go. What good could it possibly do? Life had run the way it should, had been kind to us both. She was married—the second one took, she said—still close to her kids, still interested in her work. It had been a long time ago. What had been had been. We were someone else now. And then she turned to signal to the waiter and I saw the mole by her throat, still as black as the period at the end of a sentence, and felt a small dull stab of recognition.

Standing on the corner saying our awkward goodbyes she gave my tie a quick, proprietary tug, pulled my coat closed, then gave the collar a small pat like a seal on a letter. "Was that really us?" she said.

"I hope so," I said.

She smiled, shook her head. "Take care of yourself, Tom."

She was a few stores down when she turned. "Think of me sometime," she called, an odd urgency in her voice. "Then." And she waved and went.

AND I DID, all the way down to Seventy-Second, then across Sherman Square past Gray's Papaya and the corner where the Bagel Nosh used to be, remembering the two of us crashing into each other like continents, or cats in heat, supremely self-involved. Christ, the energy we had. She'd catch a ride to the city, disappear into my room; some days, we'd hardly leave my bed. Nobody had had sex before us. We'd discovered it—it was ours alone.

My father had met her once, as we were leaving a restaurant. It was on 114th Street—windy, restless spring. He'd taken me to lunch at the Symposium, as always, because he liked to talk to the waiters in Greek. I was twenty-four, which would make him fifty. We'd just climbed the stairs up to the street when she was there, underdressed in that thin blue sweater, her hair blowing across her face. She was polite, flustered, charming, and my father said it was nice to meet her and she said it back, then looked at me and said, "So—maybe I'll see you at the library later?"

We'd almost reached the end of the block, my father with that footballer's stride of his pushing through an invisible crowd, when he smiled and said: "Now I know why I can't reach you on the phone—because you're always in the library." And maybe because I'd seen that blue sweater tangled in my sheets that morning, or because things were just different then, I said, "We're just friends, Dad—really," or something like that, and he looked at me and laughed and said, "Bullshit. What am I, blind?" and for just that moment we were closer than we'd been in years.

IT MUST HAVE been written all over us—in neon. We couldn't get enough of each other, we thought we were chosen, elect— I'm amazed I found the time to eat. My God how banal we were, and how glorious it was. How I wanted to burn her house down, how I thought about it, played with it, and how she invited it, laughing, saying, "Go ahead, burn it down, you bastard" as we walked up Amsterdam in the winter dark, her arm around my waist and her hand buried in my pocket, whispering, "Is this what you want? Like this? Take it, then, burn it, do it now."

For six months we gulped each other down, then broke up, then met again at some graduate school party from which we escaped, guiltily, after rocking the bathroom sink from the wall, then split up once more and met again a year later. Eventually, I guess, we just outran our moment.

THE CLOCK AT Grand Central gave me five minutes, and cutting through the crowd, all those intersecting lives, I found my track, my train, a seat by the window. The car lurched, settled; the platform began to move. I watched the half-lit rooms, like stage sets, going by in the dark—a heat pipe, a ladder, a chair.

BY KATONAH IT had started to snow, the small dark points, busy against the station lights, paling the sky between the hills. I'd wait all week to see her, suffocating like a fire in a closed room, and if it wasn't love, we didn't know that then. She'd come down from Manchester, I'd cancel friends, family, everything, and we'd be gone, lost, listening to the ping of the steam in the radiators, ignoring the hiss of time running out until Sunday morning when everything would begin to grow dark and miserable with the approach of her leaving and then she'd get in her friend's car and I'd walk back to my room alone.

I think even then there were times we were surprised by the force of it. Opening the door I'd see her face, her expression, shifting from need and shame to something like relief (already touched by laughter) to a desire so ragged it seemed overrun, overwhelmed, and then I'd watch that same sequence play itself out again, only altered, as in a dream, when she came, her eyes closed, her head turned almost demurely to the side, her tongue resting like some small, soft animal on her lower teeth. I wanted to close some circuit inside her, to feel her trembling in my current, and then, before we knew what had happened, we'd be holding each other by the overpass to the law school as the doughnut bags and the cigarette butts swirled in little hurricanes around our legs and her friend waited, her long fingers drumming on the wheel.

Outside the window the snowy reservoirs looked like puzzle

pieces lifted from the woods. I could see us, stepping over the missing cobbles on College Walk, my shirt half-open in the winter air, her body pressed into my ribs. That had been us. She'd said something, I'd answered. Where did we go? Did my father remember a girl, a bed, the smell of burnt onions coming from the apartment next door? Did all the moments of our days just disappear over the falls?

"BEDFORD HILLS—watch your step." I could see the snow against the cones of light, sweeping backlit past the station, and I wished it would fall and just keep falling until it buried the roads and muffled our fears and all that was left was all that mattered.

It was in January, I think. That weekend, more than any other, the thought of her leaving seemed impossible. We'd made love that afternoon, and then once more during the night when I felt her body begin to answer even before she woke and laughed and pulled me on top of her. Later, waking out of a deep, dreamless sleep I looked toward the window and realized the paling light wasn't dawn but heavy falling snow. And feeling the heat of her against me, deep in sleep, I whispered to whatever gods there might be to let it fall and just keep falling, to trap her here with me.

It was coming down hard when we woke and we lay on the mattress that we'd pulled down on the floor because the bed was too narrow, not wanting to say it out loud, watching it fall. At the Mill Luncheonette the windows were fogged and the floor was wet and the old guys at the back table who were always talking about the ponies were talking about how people had bought up all the soup and toilet paper in Morningside Heights.

Eggs and home fries had never tasted so good. Everybody was complaining, stamping around in their boots, happy. On the gray rubber mat near the door we could see the waffles of snow from people's boot soles melting. When the weather report came on, Rene, who was on the grill that morning, switched the spatula to his left and turned up the radio. It could go either way, the weather service was saying—a lot of rain or a whole lot of snow.

When we came back to my room she called her ride. They'd give it till noon, her friend said. Trying not to jinx it, she started to pack, neither of us daring to hope out loud, to think of what an extra day would mean. We could do whatever we wanted. We could ride the Staten Island Ferry, hold each other in the wind, walk up through the Village at dusk. We'd go to sleep together, walk to breakfast in the snow, go sledding on cafeteria trays with the kids in Riverside Park.

By eleven the snow had turned to rain.

And maybe because we'd allowed ourselves to think she might stay it felt like dying. There was nothing to do.

I watched her pack her things. Maybe she could stay a few hours longer, she said—take the train up, or the bus. She could say she was sick. But there was no way out. We didn't have the money for a ticket, and even if we did, it wouldn't matter. She had to go. On the street the garbage was coming up through the melting snow. She wouldn't be able to come down for two weeks. It felt like—it was—forever.

I'd already locked the door behind us when we heard the phone and we came back in and I watched her face—the disbelief, the joy so intense she had to close her eyes even as her voice spoke the necessary lies: "Oh, I'm so sorry. No, of course. I understand. No, really, it's no problem—I'm so sorry."

Her friend's great-uncle, a heart attack in Queens that morning, her ride couldn't leave till Tuesday: It seemed, it was, impossible, and then I'd caught her up and we were in each other's arms and dancing into the furniture—pardoned, disbelieving, ecstatic—but there was more, she said, her ride had to come back for the funeral the next weekend—and even as we fell into bed I remember feeling a surge of perfect, unspeakable gratitude toward this man I'd never met (who I hoped had had a long and wonderful and eventful life) for having the decency to die on that day instead of some other one and thinking, Thank you, thank you, whoever you are, and when I kick off I hope I make just enough trouble so that someone, somewhere, gets some good out of my going.

I GOT OFF THE train in Brewster, walked up the wet black stairs, the muted whistle following behind. It was snowing hard. Kate would be waiting up. I'd tell her about my day. Late that night, waking in the dark, her ribs hot against my hand, I'd hear the snow whispering something against the gutters, falling like it would never stop.

King's Cross

SOMETIMES HE COULDN'T REMEMBER A THING—not walking out of his office, not going down into the subway, not changing for the shuttle. Nothing. Just the flash of light when the train came into the upper air, the close earth banks, the sun spiking between the buildings and bodegas of Harlem. Sixteen years of stops.

The community gardens came up on the other side of the East River, ten seconds of muddy paths and raised beds pressed between the road and the tracks. Squares of turned earth. Stripes and smears of green. Now and then you'd see somebody: a bending shirt, a pair of sleeves, a pale hat. His old man started gardening around the time he got fired from the Tarrytown job. Had to have something to get holy about. Something to make you understand how much he'd lost—*Your mother and I were going to move to Vermont once*—and how it was somehow all your fault, and how he was bearing up anyway, making the best of it. Because he was stronger than you, better than you.

How many afternoons had he spent weeding the summer she got sick, listening to her hacking through the open windows?

The world darkened suddenly. Quick little spatters of rain appeared on the windows. He watched them run, thin and flat. A woman with dyed-blond hair sat frowning at a book that she held in front of her face like a mirror. A teenage girl nodding to the tiny racket of her earphones suddenly said, "I know, I know, I know," like somebody dreaming, hummed a three-note phrase and was silent. God, he'd never meant to stay here.

"Yeah? Where you goin' to go?" the old man had said to him once. "California? We still on that one? Let me ask you somethin'. What're you gonna do for money?"

They'd been over this—didn't matter what he answered.

"What, you think there's people standin' around sayin', 'Welcome to California, here's your job?' "

"No."

"That's right 'no,' so why don't you stop talkin' outta your ass and hand me that spade?" He pulled a fist-sized lettuce and tossed it toward the bucket, where it hit the side with a dull, peppery whack and started hoeing again—*slice, slice.* "When you're twenty-one you can go where you like. And you know what you'll find?" The blade hit a rock with a dull *clink.* "You'll find one place is pretty much the same as the other. You make it work or you don't. You land where you land." He looked up the row. "You call that weeded?"

"Yeah, I do—whadda *you* call it?"

It had slipped out before he knew it, but it was too late now and the blood was pounding in his ears like before a fight. He hated his father, that fat-pored nose, the crispy tufts of white hair growing out of the big brown shoulders, the way the skin on the muscles had squeezed together as if pinched by invisible fingers.

"It's weeded," he'd said, trying to keep his voice steady.

His father was looking at him. "So you're a man, now? Is that it?" He outlined their small plot with the handle of the spade. "This isn't good enough for you anymore?"

"I just—"

"Won't say no to a second helping, though—long as somebody else does the work."

He could feel the tears of frustration coming. He wanted to smash his fist into that meaty, familiar face.

"Let me tell you something. We had to make some hard choices, me and your mother. We did the best we could. When she got sick we . . ." His father looked away, his lower jaw thrust forward, his hair sticking up behind his ears. There was a smear of dirt high on his cheekbone, a bit of weed stuck to his sweating forehead. He looked like a clown, painting the air with a muddy spade. "We did the best we could," he repeated, and then, as if remembering what he'd been saying—"so we could raise a little punk who doesn't give a shit about anybody, am I right?—who just wants to wash his hands of it, who can't even help his own father pick a few tomatoes to—"

"Fuck your tomatoes," he'd yelled, his voice breaking, and running down the row he'd kicked the weed bucket so hard it flew up spinning dirt and clods like a pinwheel before landing with a single clank in the neighbor's yard.

"Fuck your tomatoes." What a great line that'd been. A long time ago now. Of course, it'd all had something to do with his mother's passing the year before—the two of them goin' at it all the time. He knew that. He remembered seeing his dad's face blurring on the other side of the hospital bed—he was still "Dad" then—and feeling like he was looking at a trapped bird smashing itself against a small cage.

Was it the last hug he'd gotten from him? Maybe. Didn't matter.

Twenty-three years. Jesus, but he could still see that bucket flyin'. It'd all unraveled after that.

The woman with the book turned a page, moving her hand from right to left as if sliding open a small window. White Plains. North White Plains. How many more before he was done? Two thousand? Three? He was shuffling toward the exit, like game night at the Garden.

When the doors opened, he stepped out. The old man's house—*his* house, once—was a five-minute walk. He should probably take a look, now that it was his again.

It'd stopped raining. He stood for a while on the wet platform. Behind him, the train spoke and the doors closed. Funny how all those years going by here he'd never seen him. A young woman in a business suit walked up the stairs and over the crosswalk. He gave her a moment, then started up.

It had started misting again, and by the time he got to the house and reached over and opened the front gate on the picket fence his face was wet. He wiped the grainy flakes of rust on his pants.

The house looked like shit—darker, older, overgrown. The

front gutter was missing, the fascia rotted and buckling, the south windows lost behind vines nobody'd bothered to cut back. He hadn't brought the keys so he looked in through the dusty windows, then sat in the rocker and looked at the garden. Weeds had taken over, though a small pile of rotting stems by the shed showed where somebody had made a halfhearted effort to keep it up. They hadn't gotten far. The lettuces had bolted, sending long purple spikes like candlesticks out of their loosened hearts. Giant cucumbers slept in the weeds. Against the fence a tomato plant, heavy with fruit, bent to the ground like a snare.

"You're a fucking mess," he said out loud.

It was still misting, though just to the north he could see rays of light cutting down between the clouds like in a religious painting. Somebody was coming up the cracked sidewalk. He started to duck down, then caught himself—it was his house. He watched as some old guy with silvery stubble on his head— Christ, was it Mr. Manetti?—walked in through the open gate, then up the overgrown walk. The old man stopped about twenty feet away. He nodded hello, then stood there with his hands deep in his pockets, looking at the house over his head. "Yours now?" he said at last.

"Guess so," he said.

"Sorry about your dad."

He didn't say anything.

"Just come by to visit?"

"Somethin' like that."

Manetti nodded. "She could use some lookin' after."

"She could. Not by me, though."

They were quiet for a few seconds.

"Should at least take some of that fruit," Manetti said. He lifted his chin toward the tomato plant. "Shame to let it rot."

He got up from the rocker. "You take it," he said. He walked down the porch steps he'd always used to jump off of as a kid, then started down the cracking drive. "Or let it rot—I really don't care."

HE'D COME HOME late after the scene in the garden, expecting a beating. When he walked in the old man was standing at the end of the hall with a washrag in his hands, his legs spread wide like he expected a wave to crash in over the living-room sofa. "Get washed up," he'd said. "Dinner's on the table."

So they ate. No grace. Some boiled beef, a few potatoes. Beans from the garden. On the table by the pushed-in chair, a wooden salad bowl filled with tomatoes.

They didn't talk. He watched him cut and spear the pieces of meat, then stab the fork into his mouth, his jaw working in small, angry circles, jabbing the next before the first was done. It had always made her crazy, the way he held the fork in his fist, hunched over his food as though worried somebody would try to take it away from him.

It was quieter than usual. He listened to his old man's knife and fork clashing like tiny swords, the knock of his glass on the wood. A car went by, then another. The clock on the wall hadn't been wound. He looked at his plate, then across the room to the window, then back to his plate.

He was half-done when the quiet from the other end of the table made him look up. His old man was looking at the table, his knife and fork like goalposts on either side of his plate. His head was tilted slightly to the side as if the table had just whispered something to him.

"Forgot the gravy," he said.

He didn't know what to say. His old man made the kind of sound a man makes when he realizes he's fucked something up: a short push of air through the mouth and nose, half-annoyed, half-amused, as if shaking his head over his own stupidity. He tried not to look at him. When the sounds of eating didn't begin, he glanced up. The goalposts were still standing. The old man was cleaning his teeth with his tongue, blinking rapidly, nodding slightly as though daring something on.

He managed to escape in time, excusing himself, almost running into the kitchen with his plate so he wouldn't have to see it. The swing-through doors flapped shut behind him. Two years later he'd left for good. Strange he'd end up living only a train stop away.

HE TURNED, walked through the town, then left at the split. He'd walk it—why not? He never walked anywhere anymore. A new subdivision, King's Cross Homes, was coming up on Mason Avenue: behind the chain link, two backhoes and an aluminum trailer sat in the mud next to the water-stained skeletons of five houses. Traffic whooshed by wetly. From a distance, the cars seemed to be trailing low, fuzzy clouds. A mile away he saw the Metro-North slipping along behind the trees. He could've been home half an hour ago. It was starting to rain again. He was surprised at how tired he was. When the road turned abruptly north, he climbed up a low, weedy embankment and set off across an L-shaped field. The scent of some kind of flower came to him in wet gusts, sickly sweet.

The truth was, he'd hardly recognized him at first. One of the guys who ran the place led him to the casket, then took two steps back and stood there with his hands folded over his crotch like he was waiting for a compliment or expecting to be kicked. There was nothing to say. There he was. He looked smaller. They'd flattened down the peak of hair on his fore-head, trapped the strands in back between his head and the white satin pillow. There was a neat bandage on his thumb, which was funny in its way: No bandage for this motherfucker.

You land where you land. Yeah, well.

Under the trees, thick with vines, the rain seemed to stop. He crossed an overgrown little meadow, raising his hands to keep them away from the waist-high nettle, then hurried, chin tucked against the rain, into the woods. He'd lost the path somewhere. It didn't matter. Ten minutes in either direction was a road.

He was following a narrow trail that turned like a stream bed around trees whose roots reached through the banks when he heard her cry out—just the word "No" followed by a short, abrupt "amah." He stopped, unsure of what he'd heard, then heard it again, followed this time by a man's voice, high and breaking: "You . . . fucking . . . bitch. How long you gonna lie to me?"

He hurried awkwardly around the turn in the trail and there they were, in the middle of a sunken clearing barely twice the size of a living room. For a moment the scene—her sobbing on the ground, her arms around her head, him standing over her, one leg on either side of her body, breathing like a spent runner—seemed unreal, like maybe they were rehearsing for something. Then the man, whose shirt had been partly pulled off his shoulder, reached down and dragged her up by the back of her jean jacket. The jacket hiked up over her neck, hunching her shoulders and sticking her arms out like a scarecrow's. Her skirt had pulled up in the back. She tried to get her feet under her but they crossed and stumbled.

"Tell me," the man yelled, his voice breaking. "Tell me—get up! Tell me!"

Her voice came from behind him, blurred. "Andy. I swear."

"I said get up."

"Please, I . . ."

"Lie to me? You gonna lie some more?" Holding her up the man raised his left hand over his right shoulder, as though pointing at something, then brought it sharp and hard across her face.

It was only after he'd yelled something and the man had stumbled, spinning around, that he realized he was drunk and noticed the bottle a few feet away in the weeds. The girl looked up from the ground, the side of her face smeared and raw. Her mouth was bleeding. Absurdly, she reached behind herself to pull down her skirt. Neither one of them was over twenty-five.

The young man smiled at him. "Get the fuck outta here. This is none a' your business."

"What're you doin'?" he said, trying to stall for time—until what, he wondered?

"This is none a' your fucking business, old man."

"What're you doing?" he said again, stupidly. He had nothing. No rocks. Nothing in his pockets. A few sticks lay on the wet ground—too short, too brittle.

"Please . . ." he heard her say.

"Shut up!" the man screamed. Then, to him: "I said get the fuck out of here."

Suddenly she was scrabbling on all fours, sobbing, twisting out of her jacket as the man grabbed for her.

Before he realized what was happening she was cowering behind him. "Please," he heard her say. "Please."

For a moment the man seemed confused. "Angela, I—" he began, and then rage changed his face as though an invisible hand had passed over it. "I told you to get the fuck out of here," he said.

"I'm just tryin' to help out," he said. He could feel her behind him, holding his sleeves like a shield.

"This is none of your fucking business."

"Listen, just . . ."

"I said get the fuck outta here." The man scooped up the empty bottle.

There was nowhere to go. For some reason he thought of his clothes. He wasn't dressed for this. The man was holding the bottle loose like a knife. Behind them was the waist-high bank. There was nowhere to go.

"Wait," he said. He felt a small bump and knew she'd backed up against the dirt. "Wait—"

"I swear to God I'll kill you."

"Is that what you want?" he said suddenly.

The man was still moving toward him, holding the bottle out from his body.

"Look at me. What would you win? I'm old enough to be your father."

Something stuttered in the man's eyes.

"Why're you so angry?"

To his amazement the man's eyebrows gathered and his chin stuck out as though he was confused about something yet determined to think it through. He glanced quickly to the left, raised the bottle, then lowered it. He blinked once, then again—and began to cry. "You don't understand," he said. He waved the bottle vaguely. "You don't understand. I just—" He put his fingers to the bridge of his nose like a man who's been working too hard. "Oh, fuck," he said, then started to laugh, the sobs shaking his body. "Oh, fuck."

"Danny?" he heard the woman whisper, letting go of his sleeves.

"Listen, if you want you can come with . . ." he began, but she shook her head.

He watched her cross the clearing and awkwardly put her arms around the man as he crouched on his heels in the dirt.

After a second he walked over and touched the man's shoulder.

"Time to go home, son," he said.

Russian Mammoths

I THINK IT WAS THE BUDDHISTS WHO DIVIDED life into four parts, reserving the last—after the kids, after the stuff—for enlightenment. The search for it. Who said you have to walk out on the road with just a bowl and a blanket. Throw yourself before the world's mercy. Imagine it. To the end of your days. The bite of smoke in the wind, the small rain on your bald head.

No wheedling, no bargaining with "revenant, white-faced death," as Horace put it, no advertising your memories in the pennysaver like so many commemorative beer steins—nothing. Close up, pull out. Leave it where it stands. God knows it has its appeal. But the stuff sticks. And the stuff that sticks to the stuff sticks. And the smell of a childhood drawer can bring me to tears. And there are times since she went, I'll be honest, when loss is the only language I hear.

Everything's taken from us anyway. Without mercy. To give it away is like saying you quit just before you're fired.

———

I'D HAVE TO say I didn't know the little girl, really. Or her mother, for that matter. Just one of the Ecuadorian kids—six, seven, eight years old—waiting by the fence for the bus every morning. Climbing up on the low wall, holding on to the pickets. I tried some of my idiot's Spanish on them—*Estos son mis flores—te gusta?*—until I realized they were just shy. Nice kids. For years now every April I put in a row of Russian Mammoths along the fence, thinking that even after they'd moved on and the world had done its work they might still remember flowers three times their height. Waiting for the bus, the white fence in the still, hot sun, and flowers three times their height.

They must have been doing well to afford dance lessons. It was the new place, across from Borden's Bridge. Driving by sometimes I'd see the little ones through the big front windows, taking turns. They had just closed the door behind them when Eduardo Machado took his. Or missed it, I guess you could say. Minutes later, up on Prospect Street, I heard the sirens. I was pulling up the vines, piling the tomato stakes in the grass. It's something I enjoy: Exposing the dirt to the sky again, that peppery smell, like a bit of August, released; the indulgence of small regrets. Under the tangles the old fruit had left stains of tomato seeds on the dirt and bits of orange skin, parchment dry.

It doesn't add up to much, really. They'd watch me weed sometimes, or transplant beans from the pots. When I had it to give I'd give them a bit of cilantro or basil to smell, their brown hands, like sea anemones, reaching through the fence, or show them how to pinch the suckers off the tomatoes. Sometimes they'd be interested; sometimes not. In September I'd bend the sunflowers down, clear the rubbery pollen off with my thumb and let them scrape the seeds into their palms, and every year the veterans, shoving up to the front, would show the newcomers how to pry them out of their shiny black ranks and crack out the tiny white tongues of meat. I'd always deadhead the Mammoths at night because they don't fall like flowers but topple and crash, and walking down the line once, lopping off the two-pound heads with the shears, I saw them watching me.

This fall I made myself carve some pumpkins, figuring it was time. I did a good job. Tragedy and Comedy, with fangs. I can see them both from where I sit, pulling in their cheeks, collapsing on the warm wood of the porch. Funny how we try to scare ourselves with the claws, the fangs . . . You want to frighten yourself, carve something you love, then watch what happens.

The chair feels loose against my back; I'll have to look at it one of these days. I don't know what to do, really. It's like I can't breathe suddenly, yet there's air all around. It's not like I believed in much these past years. Something, I thought. Now I don't know. I can't tell you if they'll be back in front of my house Monday morning, and if they are, if I'll have the strength to look through my own living-room window, and if I do, if I'll be able to stand what I see; if it will be the bossy one missing, or the one who always stands by the corner with her mother, or the one who scraped her knee on the wall last spring . . . The paper had their names, but the truth is I didn't know their names.

IT WAS A beautiful evening, beautiful: Calm, appropriately chill for early November, the sky above the hills steeping through the range of blues to black; I remember noticing how cold my fingers felt and thinking how good it was to work and that tonight, finally, we might get our frost. I could hear the cars down the hill, and then a while later the train. At some point the sirens started, then stopped, and I heard the bells from the church and then sirens again and when I looked up it was dark and I couldn't tell the sky from the hill anymore.

The world doesn't care for us—we pass through its rooms like ghosts. You can hear it, sometimes, laughing, celebrating, and when we take our leave it's no more than the shift of air through an open door that someone forgot to close. And I ask you, what was the point—of the smell of basil, the pumpkins, the building up of love? Tell me. And where do we go? And how could it possibly be forever? And who could blame the person who, seeing how it is, simply refuses to play?

IT WAS JOHN, out on his recovery walk, who told me, though if I'd seen him first I suppose I might not have heard at all. I've gotten pretty good at avoiding them, the baggy one with the huge earphones, the one who walks as if his body were borrowed, the one who always looks confused. They're always walking— carefully, somehow, like snails testing the air for something familiar—away from whoever it is they were, I guess. Half-pardoned. I've learned to check before I leave the porch, pretend not to hear when they call my name. I've never been completely sure where they come from. If the same faces didn't repeat you'd swear they'd filled the world by now, a river out of Brewster.

Everyone's figured it out but John. Whenever John sees me

he'll call out in that over-hearty, "talking to people is part of your therapy" voice and just stand there until I can't stand it and have to turn and be surprised to see him standing there and he'll say, "How's the garden coming sure looks good from here" or "How about that Obama, you think he can hold on?" and we'll chat inanely about tomatoes or the venality of the Republican Party until I say, "Well, gotta get back . . ." and he'll say, "Well, bye for now," and then we do it again the next time.

This morning I looked but everything seemed fine. I didn't see him until he was right there, damn near on top of me. I started to turn around, instinctively, and then, trying to cover up, called out, "Good morning, John, little chilly this morning, isn't it?" and he said, "Sure is, but what're you gonna do?" And then, "Terrible what happened last night, isn't it?" about how some Mexican lady and her daughter had been killed by an illegal as they were coming out of the dance studio across from the bridge, the new place, did I know it? and I said yes, and he said well, right there.

"Real shame," he said. "For a while they thought the mother might make it."

"What happened?" I said.

"Couldn't save her, I guess."

"No, I mean . . ."

"Oh. Pretty much what you'd expect." He made his hand into a wobbling jug and guzzled from the thumb, and at that moment—this is what a coward the mind is—I remember thinking that I'd seen people use the same gesture, without the wobbling, to describe talking on the phone, speaking into their pinkie, and thought, drinking—a kind of calling, I suppose, for some, and if the phone wobbled would it be a drunk making a call? . . . and only then returned to his voice saying, "Like he didn't see the turn at all. Goin' so fast he put half the car in the studio."

"Jesus Christ," I said.

"Pretty terrible, all right. I heard they lived just over here, on Nooner. Strange, right? You and I probably saw them a hundred times. Maybe a thousand times."

"Yeah," I said.

John looked at the browning vines of the morning glories wound into the fence. For a terrible moment I thought he was going to say something about the garden. "I heard he just sat there," he said.

I looked at him.

"I mean when the cops got there," he said. "The guy. Sirens everywhere, cops are yellin' for him to get out of the car, and he just sits there, perfectly calm. Like he's trying to remember something he had to do. When they opened the door he threw up."

He shook his head, as if disagreeing with something. "Terrible thing, but what're you gonna do, right?"

"Not much," I said.

"Boy, you got that right." And then: "Well, I guess I better be going."

"Yeah," I said.

He was halfway down the fence when he turned around. "Hey, maybe you can bring some of these flowers down there. I mean, you should see it down there. They got those, you know, what do you call 'em, those cement kind of things you see by the highway all set up."

"Barricades."

"Can't even see 'em anymore, all the stuff people have brought." He paused, then raised his hand like a Hollywood Indian, absurd to the last: "Well, bye for now."

AND WHAT WOULD I do there, my recovering friend? Shake my head, offer my opinion? Shall I say a prayer over the shards? Lay my hand on the splintered studs? It's all makeup, all of it. The child is dead, she doesn't need my flowers, and God doesn't deserve them.

It's done. The cops have hosed off the pavement, pulled the pocketbook out of the weeds. There's nothing to do. If there were any justice left it would shrivel and die at the injustice of it all and all you can think to do is go out and buy a drugstore dinosaur and stand around with that sad mime look on your face, that respectful museumgoer's look on your face, listening to the guy from the Kiwanis Club and the three-hundred-pound checkout girl from the A&P go on about how just the other day, and if only they'd thought, and why them, of all people, all the time wondering if you've stayed long enough and whether it's OK to check your phone.

I've seen it before: the low wave of bubblegum-colored trash, the semi-literate messages tacked to the plywood—"We Love You, Well Always Remmember You," the mothers with their stick-on nails . . . and I don't think I can stand it again, I want to take a shovel to your heads you liars, how soon you'll forget her, how soon you always forget—a year from now you won't remember her name. No, you want to bring something, bring something you'll remember: Bring the unwashed hood and bolt it to the pavement; bring an arm and lay it down.

A LIGHT RAIN this morning. Now it's still, gray, the season clamping tight. I couldn't sleep last night, or read. . . . Sometime after three I walked out on the porch and the sky was still clear and I could see the dark bulk of the hill above the tracks and I just stood there in my shirt, letting myself be cold. As I turned to go back I noticed the pumpkins on the top step, but when I tried to pick one up my thumb punched right through the cold pulp to the space inside and I thought to myself, I have to take them out to the compost pile, I have to take them out with the ashes and the kitchen trash.

That numbness, that feeling of being outside the world—I hadn't expected to know it again, to feel something slowly suffocating in your chest and yet to feel as if it's not your chest at all. . . . To see your hands holding the paper, washing your bowl. I hadn't planned on missing her again. My baby.

IT WAS LATE afternoon that I carried them out to the back. A cold day. I had to take them one at a time, holding them underneath where the meat still held and carry them around, the fangs gone soft, the cheeks purpled with rot, the eyes collapsed to slits. I placed the first one down by the heap, then went back for the second, trying not to look at it. When I set it down a soft black cloud of midges came from around the stem-top opening and I just swung the shovel and cleaved it in half, then again, and again, with the flat and then the blade, slicing eye from eye, crushing them back into pulp, into nothing, into nothing we could ever recognize or know, crying like a child now because yes, there are times when the world's too much no matter how long you live.

And I dropped the shovel and picked up the fork and stabbed it into the waist-high hill to make a space and at that moment the hot heart of the pile breathed out into the cold—a sigh of dark loam and ashes and leaves and turning rot—unbidden, undeserved, like a last sob before sleep.

August

WHEN I THINK BACK ON OUR FIVE SEASONS AT THE LAKE, I see my father reading in the big wicker chair that usually stood in the corner under the lamp with the green shade but which he'd drag in front of the fire on chilly days. He was a great reader, my father: at ease, engaged, capable of sitting for three hours at a stretch without feeling the need to get up or move about, almost immobile except for now and again a small inward smile or a slight tilt of the head in anticipation of the page's turning. Sometimes I'd see his arm swing like a crane to the little table at his side. He'd pick up the glass with three fingers, begin to bring it to his lips—all this without once looking up from the page—and stop. And the glass would just hang there, sometimes for a minute or more, and I'd make bets with myself on whether it would complete its journey by the time he got to the bottom of the page or be returned, untouched, to the table.

My mother read too, though differently. For days or weeks she would read nothing at all, or nothing but the newspaper, then suddenly take a book off the shelf, pull a chair next to my father's, and disappear. She read with an all-absorbing intensity that I understood completely and yet still found slightly unnerving, her stockinged feet drawn up underneath her. Hunched over the book—which she'd hold tight to her stomach, forcing her to look straight down—she'd look like she was protecting the thing, or in pain. No smile, no cup of tea, no leg thrown easily over the other—this was less a dance than a battle of some kind, though what was being fought for, or by whom, I could hardly guess. Two days after it had begun—during which time my mother would often drag a chair out to the shore after breakfast, or retire to one of the hammocks my father had strung about the place, in which she would lie, straight-legged, smoking cigarettes, holding the book above her head—it would be over. I would find her lying in the hammock, staring up into the trees, the book tossed on the grass beside her.

It was in our second season on the lake that my father shot the dog with Mr. Colby's gun and Mrs. Kessler fell in love with the man who lived in the cabin on the other side of the lake. He was much younger than she was, which was very important, and everyone talked about it those two weeks whenever they thought I couldn't hear, changing the subject to food or asking me if I'd seen the heron by the dam as soon as I came closer. She'd made a spectacle of herself, which made me think of glasses even though I knew what it meant, and really it was a bit much, this carrying on in plain view. Everyone seemed angry about it, and though my parents and the Mostovskys and some of the others didn't have much to say, I could always tell when people were talking about it by the way they would look slightly off to the side, shaking their heads, or the way they'd shrug their shoulders, like they didn't care, or the way some would lean forward while others, giving their opinion, would lean back luxuriously in their Adirondack chairs.

I knew it was probably wrong and shameful for a married lady to fall in love with somebody, and particularly somebody younger, but the truth is that I liked Mrs. Kessler. She'd come across me once while I was working on one of my many forts in the woods and kept my secret, and sometimes when Harold Mostovsky and I spent the long, hot afternoons feeling around in the water with our toes, trying to walk the pasture walls that had disappeared when the lake was made, we would look up to see her sitting on the shore watching us, her arms around her legs, and when she saw we'd seen her, she'd give a hesitant little wave, raising her hand a bit, then a bit more, as though not sure how high she should bring it, and we'd go back to what we were doing. It never bothered us having her there, and then at some point we'd look up and she'd be gone.

Though I never saw it myself, I was told Mrs. Kessler lost her head so completely that at night she'd walk down to the lake just an hour or two after dusk and get into the rowboat and row across to the other man's cabin while Mr. Kessler sat reading by the green lamp in their cabin. (I wonder what Kessler's reading, I heard Mr. Černý say. Must be good.) That she'd sometimes stay for hours and hours, not caring what anybody thought, and that Mrs. Eugenia Bartlett had sworn she'd heard the creak of her oarlocks as she rowed back through the mist early one morning just before dawn.

My mother, I remember, seemed almost lighthearted that

second week in June, waking early, surprising me with special meals like apricot dumplings and kašička with drops of jam, asking my father about things in the newspaper. She threw out the stacks of magazines and junk that had collected under the sink and swept out the cobwebs and the bottle caps and the mouse droppings that looked like fat caraway seeds and the bits of mattress stuffing and lint from last winter's nests. One fresh morning after a night of rain she came home with the trunk of the DeSoto crammed with planting trays and seeds and bags of soil and fertilizer and sixteen hanging flowerpots and a paper bag with sixteen hooks to hang them on. In the backseat of the car were four carton bottoms filled with flowers. Except for the marigolds, I didn't know their names. Some were purple and white, like pinwheels, others a dark velvety red, still others the color of the sky just before it gets dark. They seemed to soak in the spotted light that came through the windows, trembling with life. She was going to garden, my mother said.

I saw my father looking at my mother as she pointed out to us all the things she'd bought, then started to drag one of the cartons out of the car. Here, let me get that, he said.

We carried the cartons down to the shady, tangled grass by the water, placing them side by side so they made a long, lovely rectangle, then returned for the bags of soil and the tools. It was midmorning. The air was warming quickly. A few people had gathered out on the float in the middle of the lake, and we could hear them laughing. My father carried out the card table my mother said she wanted to work on, and for the next few hours, while my father drilled holes into the south wall of the cabin and screwed the hooks into them, my mother and I transplanted the flowers into the hanging pots, filled the seed flats with soil, and sprinkled the tiny seeds from the packets into furrows we made in the dirt with the eraser end of a pencil. When my father was finished he asked if there was anything else my mother wanted him to do, but she said no, that he'd done a wonderful job with the hooks and that we could do the rest on our own, couldn't we, and I agreed.

My mother talked more that morning than I could remember her talking in a long time. She asked me about school and said how happy she was we had a cabin on a lake and how she hadn't liked it at first because it reminded her too much of home but that she saw things differently now and loved it as much, no, in some ways even more than the countryside she had known as a little girl. And she told me a little bit about the war and what that had been like, and about a certain square in Prague with benches and flower beds and giant twisted oaks, and how she still remembered that square as well as a certain churchyard a few minutes away, and when a particular burst of laughter carried over the water she looked at me and said, "People can be silly, can't they, complicating their lives for no reason, don't ever complicate your life, promise me that," and though I didn't know what she meant, I said I wouldn't. Later, as we were planting the pinwheel flowers in the new pots, pressing down the soil with our fingers so the roots would take, she told me she'd made some mistakes in her life but that it was never too late to understand things and that she understood things now and that she had never been happier than she was at that moment. She suggested we take a break for lunch, but later, when I found her in the hammock, smoking, she said she was a little tired, and it wasn't until the next day that we finished and by that time some of the flowers in the cartons, which we'd forgotten to water, had wilted badly.

I was reading in my room that evening after dinner when I heard my mother get up from the wicker chair and go into the kitchen. I heard the refrigerator door open and close, then the quick clink of glass against glass. I heard the water in the sink, then the creak of the wicker again. "What time is it?" she asked my father.

It took a second for my father to move his book to his left hand and, holding his place with his finger, push up the sleeve of his sweater. "Half past nine," he said.

"Almost time for him to go to bed," my mother said. There was no answer. A few minutes later she was up once more.

"You think she'll do it again?" she said from somewhere by the window.

"I think she might," my father said in his I'm-reading voice.

"What could she be thinking?" said my mother.

"Pretty much what you'd expect, I imagine."

"I don't think it's just that."

"I never said it was."

"Time for bed," my mother called. I pretended I couldn't hear. "What's he doing in there?" said my mother, and walking over, she knocked on the wood plank door to my room. "Bedtime," she said. They were quiet for a few moments.

"She's a fool," said my mother. "I thought she had more sense, throwing everything away like this."

They were quiet for a long time.

"I don't know that you want to stand by the window like that," my father said.

"I'm not the one who has to worry about being seen. And Kessler," she said, after a moment. "Him I can't understand."

"What would you have him do?"

"Something. Anything."

Again they were quiet. I heard a page turn.

"And for what?" she went on after a while. "Nothing."

"I don't imagine she sees it that way," said my father.

"You don't?"

"No."

"How does she see it then?"

"Differently."

"So you're saying there's nothing wrong with him sitting there reading like an idiot while his wife . . ."

"I didn't say that."

"Christ, you're understanding."

"Am I?"

"You go to hell."

I heard my father get out of the wicker chair, then whisper something I couldn't make out: "I've never asked . . . little enough . . . to blame . . . fault." And then I heard my mother crying and my father saying, "All right, there, come now, everything's all right."

THE NEXT MORNING my mother woke me while everything was still cool and fresh. She had made a big plate of palačinky so light and thin you could see the bruise of the jam through the sides of the crepes. She'd set out two deck chairs in the middle of the old garden plot, she said, we could eat breakfast outside—a special treat. She put the palačinky on a tray with two cups of sweetened tea and together we walked up the steps away from the lake to the garden, where we sat under light blankets with the weeds and the thistles growing up all around us and ate with our fingers, draping the floppy crepes between our thumbs and pinkies so the preserves wouldn't come out and feeding them into our mouths. We laughed about dumb things and pretended to call out to a waiter who stood in the old strawberry patch and to be frustrated when we couldn't catch his eye.

"What do you think he's doing?" my mother said.

"He's not paying attention to us," I said. I waved my arms wildly, as if signaling a boat far offshore.

"Careful," my mother said.

I put my cup of tea on its saucer down on the ground, making a space between the long grasses. I waved my arms again. "Can I get some more jam?" I called out. "And some hot chocolate, please?"

My mother was looking at the overgrown strawberry patch as though a man actually stood there in the weeds. "What do you suppose he's thinking about?" she said, as if to herself.

I didn't know what to say.

"I think he's thinking about a girl," my mother said. She was looking at the strawberry patch. A small breeze moved the patches of shade and sun on the ground, then returned them to where they had been. She laughed strangely. "I don't think we can get his attention."

"Why don't we throw something at him," I said, and, leaning over, I picked up a short, thick branch and sent it flying through the air above the strawberry patch. It fell in the weeds at the far end of the garden. "Missed," I said. I reached for another stick. "This time I'll . . ."

"He's smoking," said my mother. "Look at the way he brings it to his mouth. The way he stands with his elbows back on the bar."

I looked at her, wanting to follow her, to play on this new field she was making.

"I bet he gets in trouble," I said.

She nodded slowly, agreeing with something I hadn't said. "I don't think he's the kind of man who would care very much. I don't think he'll care at all." She looked around the dead garden, then shook her head and smiled as if remembering an old joke. "So here we are. Nothing to do but call for the check."

My mother worked on her flowers all that afternoon, sitting at the wooden table in the shade, a cup of coffee and a cigarette next to her, cupping big handfuls of black soil with her hands from the small mountain she'd spilled on the wood next to her, packing the pots, then making a space for the root ball by pushing the dirt to the side with her fingers the way a potter shapes the sides of a vase. I went off to play for a while, then returned to find her sitting with her elbows on the table. She was holding the cigarette and the cup of coffee in her right hand as though just about to pick them up, and her head was tilted slightly to the side. She was looking at a spot on the grass a short distance away.

I didn't want to disturb her so I sat down quietly on the wooden steps to wait until she started working again. Everything was still. Far across the water a group of kids I didn't know were jumping from the children's dock into the water. Their little screams sounded strangely distant, as though I were hearing them from inside a closed room.

My father spoke from the open bedroom window. "Can I get you something?" His voice was very close, but though I knew he was right there, I couldn't see him: the angle made the screen opaque as a wall.

"No," my mother said. She didn't look up.

"Something to eat? A cup of tea?" In the other room, the children screamed happily. I could see them run down the hill and onto the slightly lopsided dock, then spear into the water. They looked like little white sticks.

"No," my mother said again. And then, after a long while: "Thank you."

IT WAS NOT long afterward—three days, maybe a week—that my father shot the dog. Harold Mostovsky and I heard it first while we were exploring along the brook one quiet, cloudy morning: a furious, concentrated thrashing in the underbrush. There was no other sound, I remember—no growling or snarling. When we came closer we thought at first what we were seeing was two dogs, then a shepherd with something around its neck. Only when it sank its teeth in its own tail and bayed in pain, then bit its own hind leg, did we realize something was wrong. And terrified of this thing trying to kill itself, we began to run.

I never thought to ask him how he knew. Whether someone had called him, or whether he'd been walking in the area, or whether he'd somehow simply sensed it, the way parents sometimes will. All I know for certain is that he and old Ashby, who lived in a shack a mile away and who always wore overalls and a sleeveless T-shirt, were suddenly there, and my father was yelling, "Whose? Where?" then running for the old white Colby house, which stood on a little rise a hundred yards away. As Harold and I ran up behind them I heard my father ask, Do you know where he keeps the shells? then saw him tap the bottom right pane with his elbow and reach in and open the door. A moment later he was walking out with the shotgun. He brought it up to his face, studying it quickly, then broke it and chambered a red shell he took from his pocket. "Stay here," he told us.

The shepherd was still there. It was trying to get at its stomach. It had bitten off its own tail; the stub ended in a small, pink circle. It seemed to be trying to stand on its right shoulder. It had shit all over itself and the smell was terrible. My father walked right over to it, extended the gun, and shot it in the head. At the sound of the two-part crash the dog fell to the ground like a dropped rubber toy; I caught a glimpse of what had been its head—a grinning jaw of teeth, a mat of fur, something pink like a thumb—and then my father's body blocked the view and he was turning us gently around. "Go home," he said. "This is not for you. Go on." And then, to Ashby: "Get the shovel. I would like to take care of this quickly."

And that was all, really. My father didn't talk about it much, except to ask if I was all right and to explain that the dog had gotten into some poison some idiot had left out and that the thing had had to be done. He seemed strangely happy that week, unburdened. It started to rain that same afternoon, and when the water began to spill over the sides of the leaf-clogged gutter in long, wavering sheets that tore open to show the trees and the hill, then sewed themselves up again, he took off his shirt and shoes and walked hatless into the downpour and unclogged the pipe and dug at the mats of blackened leaves gathered against the back of the cabin with his hands and carried them against his soaking chest into the woods.

It rained for three days. Soon after it stopped, Mr. and Mrs. Kessler left the lake because Mrs. Kessler was in love with the man who lived in the cove and wouldn't listen to reason. I never saw them again. The man stayed on for a while—we could see him row out to the dock and swim by himself in the evenings just before dark—as though he didn't want to go or thought she might come back, but then he left too. My mother kept gardening, and for a time the south side of the cabin burst into color: waterfalls of blossoms cascaded against the wood and bouquets filled with air moved sluggishly in the afternoon heat, but by late August something had gone wrong and they began to die and my mother lost interest. My father made a halfhearted effort to keep them up but they died anyway, and one day he took the pots off the wall and dumped the soil out of them in a corner of the old garden then came back down and unscrewed the hooks out of the cabin wall and got a small brush and painted the white insides of the holes with dark stain so they couldn't be seen. The sixteen pots of soil looked like cake molds, white with roots, and they lay there until my father broke them up with a spade and spread them out into the weeds.

Justice

IN MAY 1968, RUSSIAN TANKS HADN'T ROLLED into Prague yet, my mother hadn't gone crazy, and out on Route 22, just down from the dairy farm that's now a Carpet Warehouse, Sam's Bait and Tackle held a fishing contest.

I was ten and awkward in that first-generation, white-shirt-and-black-bread-sandwich way, my squareness reinforced by my every attempt to be hip, my brown Oxfords and no-nonsense crew cut redeemed, but only slightly, by a modest athleticism and a certain willingness to get beat up if the situation called for it. I didn't like football, though I pretended to. I didn't care about baseball, though I could pitch a little. I'd noticed girls but couldn't talk to them. In the pictures I seem to be listening for something, wanting to smile but not sure I should.

My great passion was fishing. Though we lived in Queens, my parents rented a cabin on a lake for the summers, and it was done. This wasn't a hobby. I could tell you which part of China the Tonkin cane came from that craftsmen like Hiram Leonard and Jim Payne turned into split-bamboo fly rods I could never afford. I could tell you what size and pattern of terrestrial to use in August on the legendary Letort Creek in Pennsylvania, though I'd never been within a hundred miles of it. I read Ernest Schwiebert and Art Flick, pored over *Field & Stream* with Talmudic concentration, spent hours tying my own trout flies while listening to Cousin Brucie in the darkroom where my dad hid his vodka in rinsed-out bottles of fixative.

And every summer I fished my heart out, lifting up the latch on the kitchen door and sneaking out into the morning fog, pouring water over my head at noon, flailing around after dark, a thousand bullfrogs roaring in my ears. If this was a kind of love, it was no sillier than most and better than many, and I devoted myself to it as I've devoted myself to few things in this life. All I had to do was keep at it, and things would come out right: the odds would kick in, the surface would shatter, and I'd know I'd summoned something extraordinary, something few others had seen or imagined. The knot would hold, because I'd earned it.

What I'm saying is that fishing mattered to me then. Walking to PS 206 in the cold, the brown buildings of LeFrak City fading in the sleet, I'd imagine my Jitterbug gurgling placidly along a mossy log, the wake of something dark rising up behind it. All through December and January, February, and March I'd sit in my room with a plate of my mother's bábovka, curled up like a moth in its chrysalis, dreaming. And then, just like that, the loaf-shaped hedges along Sixty-Third Road would be green and we'd be driving across the Triborough Bridge and up the Saw Mill River Parkway, winding back the season until, somewhere around Bedford, only the willows showed any color.

There'd be a protocol. We'd always stop at the Red Rooster, where my father would buy me a strawberry milkshake while my mother stayed in the car, and coming up Doansburg Road, whichever one of us first spotted the Green Chimneys school, or Schlump's mailbox, or the post office, would get to yell *Školka!*, or *Schlump!*, or *Pošta!*, and then we'd be there, pushing open the swollen door, breathing in that sharp, dank cedar smell, touching all the sleeping things, remembering ourselves to them.

Most years we wouldn't move out to the cabin until school let out, but that year my parents took me out of school a month early. Things were complicated, my mother told me. Daddy would probably stay in the city—he taught at Columbia—and come up on the weekends. Things were complicated there too—at Columbia—he needed to do what he could. But it was fine. Everything was fine. The two of us would be moving back home to Czechoslovakia that fall. She'd waited long enough, and though Daddy didn't always agree, sometimes you had to take a risk, sometimes you had to take a chance at happiness because life just flew by and then it was gone and what was the point of it all if not to be happy and among your own? When we moved she'd show me the lakes she'd known as a little girl. Beautiful lakes. Full of carp and pike—huge fish. We had family there— aunts, uncles. I'd have so many friends there.

DADDY DIDN'T HAVE the nerve. He didn't believe in dubček, which I thought was a kind of luck. He didn't know what it was like to slowly suffocate while he waltzed off to his classes to play the big man in front of all those graduate students in their miniskirts. But once we'd made the move, he'd understand, and join us. It would be like it used to be—maybe not perfect, but right.

I'd been asleep in my room when their voices closed my dreams.

"You know that's not true," I heard my father say—"I want this as much as you do."

My mother laughed—a short, sharp laugh like a cough.

"You? It's all the same to you—here, there . . ."

"That's ridiculous."

I could hear the water, the touch and clink of dishes. My father, I knew, would be standing in the kitchen doorway; she'd be by the sink, her white arms disappearing in the long, yellow gloves.

"Every day it's take off your hat, read the paper, shovel your dinner—I could put ashes on your plate you wouldn't know the difference."

"So this is about how I eat now? I'm just saying this isn't some fairy tale you decide to believe in because . . ."

"We're going. I don't care—"

"Obviously—"

"We never fucking said it would be forever, we—"

"Keep your voice down, he's—"

"We're going home, and you can come with us or sit here and . . . rot."

"Six months."

"No."

"That's all I'm asking."

"No."

"If it holds—"

Something smashed and a second later my door opened and my dad came in and closed it quickly behind him and came and sat on my bed in the dark. Had they woken me? It was nothing. I should go to sleep, everything would be fine. And he pet my head with his heavy hand until I pretended to be asleep. He smelled like smoke.

AND SO MOM and I went to the lake before we moved to Czechoslovakia and Daddy stayed in the city. I don't know if it was hard for him. When I imagine him then, I see him sitting up late in our apartment, the sweat quietly running down his back, listening to the drone of the expressway. Wondering if she was right.

At the time, I didn't think about him much at all. My best friend, Matt, had moved away that spring, and the lake was almost empty because people didn't really come up till June, but Mom and I were fine. It was still cold so we made fires in the fireplace every night and slept under hills of blankets and talked through the wooden wall between our rooms and laughed. Mom kept a hammer and a knife under her bed just in case somebody tried to break in.

I'd be up so early the lake would still be invisible, a mirror in the fog. I liked seeing how quiet I could be, pulling my jeans on slowly, not stirring the tea till I was outside. Mom would sleep in, then read in bed till noon. She was still Mom, then. The day would pass in a slow waltz, me off in the boat, Mom reading in the hammock in the watery shade, the two of us drifting together to eat, or to swim. The shadows would shrink into the eastern shore, the sun rise on its arc, the shadows grow from the west.

Twice a day she'd come down to admire the fish I caught, which I'd pull up for her, their red gills flaring and closing in the heat, and I'd tell her about the one that had broken my line and she'd say I'd catch an even bigger one next time, and then we'd walk up through the long, knotted grass to the cabin. She was my best friend.

It wasn't long after we came to the cabin that year that I saw the sign scotch-taped to the wooden counter at Sam's. The contest was for the biggest bass officially weighed in by six p.m. on June 1, and the winning prize—there was no second or third— was two hundred dollars in store credit. I didn't think about it much. This wasn't for me—this was for grown-ups. Already the fish in the lead, a nineteen-inch trophy weighing four pounds, three ounces—caught by a man who looked like my math teacher, Mr. Wentzel—was three inches longer than the biggest bass I'd ever seen.

I looked at the picture of Mr. Wentzel holding his fish out to the camera, then picked some five-cent plastic worms from the candy jars on the counter while the owner, a thin man with a big Adam's apple who always seemed about to be angry, watched me over the top of the reel he was filling with monofilament by the cash register. "Back again?" he'd say whenever I came in to buy some worms, and I'd say, "Yes, sir," and he'd say, "Just make sure you put all those back," and go back to what he was doing.

My mom, who'd been crying in the hammock when I came in for lunch that day, saw me looking at the picture. *To je macek*, she said, leaning in for a closer look: That's a whopper.

I nodded.

Kluku, mělbys to zkusit, she said—You should try it, kiddo.

I shrugged.

"Don't you think he should try it?" she said to the owner, who was winding the reel while holding a cigarette.

He didn't hear her.

"I think he could win, don't you?"

"What is that, German?" he said.

"I'm sorry?"

"Whatever it is you're always talkin'."

"It's Czech."

"What's that?"

"Not German."

He cut the line with a pair of scissors, then put a fat rubber band on the spool to keep the line from unwinding. "Why don't you just talk English, where people could understand you?"

"I am speaking English."

He smiled and tilted his head a little like something hadn't gone down right, then nodded toward the contest sign. "Open to anybody with a license," he said. He picked up another reel. "Could buy himself a lifetime supply of those plastic worms."

"Yes, he could," my mother said, and the man looked up at her, took a drag, then turned back to his reel.

I WAS UP early that morning, like every morning, dropping the latch quietly behind me, stowing my gear behind the wooden seat, rowing with short, choppy strokes to keep the oarlocks from creaking till I couldn't see the shore. The air wet my face and somewhere out in the fog some jays started up and then stopped and everything was still. I fished by ear, mostly, casting the weedless frog out into the mist, listening for a strike. Near the cabin where Matt used to live I got a 14-inch bass, the biggest I'd caught in a while, then nothing. It was strange seeing his dock and knowing he wasn't coming back there, and I wondered if someone would think the same thing about me. I fished on. At some point, the mist began to yellow and the very tops of the oaks came out. When I looked again, a dark fringe of leaves floated high above the lake and the fog over my head had thinned to a cloudy blue like an old dog's eyes.

I could make out bits of the shoreline now, and I cast my Amazin' Weedless Frog out over the dark water toward the fallen trees, then hopped it back and cast again. And again. A quick, white sun lit the trees on the western shore, disappeared.

Not far from the four cedar boards that made our dam I cast the frog into the shallows, let it sit, then scurried it over the open water onto a plate-sized mat of ropy weeds. And then the water erupted and the mat of weeds disappeared into a red-gilled, rattling maw big enough to fit my head into, and I hauled back on the rod and set the hook.

How I managed to get that bass into the boat, I have no idea, but I did. It took a while. I had no net. Toward the end, shifting the straining rod to my left hand, I reached down into the water and pinned a huge clump of weeds to the side of the boat; inside it I could feel a gill plate wider than my hand. Disbelieving, I wallowed the monster, still encased in weeds, into the rowboat and started to scream.

My mother, hearing me yell, came running down to the

dock, barefoot, holding her nightgown above the long grass. The bass, with its huge, underslung white belly, measured just under twenty-six inches long and probably weighed eight or nine pounds. We were laughing and yelling in disbelief, jumping around on the wooden boards of the dock, and then we looked at each other and we were in the car and Mom, still in her thin nightgown, was driving down Fairfield Drive where the American Nazi Party used to march long before I was born and I was sitting with the bass headfirst in a metal bucket of water, its tail slapping against the glove compartment.

We skidded into the gravel parking lot and I was out and running, hugging the sloshing bucket. I could hear my mother, slumped down in the seat, shouting encouragement out the window, cheering me on.

I can still see him, writing something by the cash register. He's just opened up—another day on this sinking ship, which he never wanted in the first place, which was his brother-in-law's idea—when the door flies open and that little Kraut kid comes staggering in carrying a bucket with a tail flopping a full foot over the rim. This isn't possible. He's got Pete with the picture all lined up to go.

I didn't see him look up—I was working too hard carrying the bucket. He was writing something on a pad.

"Caught a fish, huh?" he said. There was no one else in the store.

I don't remember what I babbled: "A huge one," "The biggest fish I ever saw"—it doesn't matter.

"Well, good for you." He flipped the page, then flipped it back. I didn't understand what was happening.

"So . . . what can I do for you today?"

"The contest," I said, like an idiot. "The bass contest. I—"

He looked up from the pad, distracted, irritated.

"The bass contest," I explained. "I thought—"

"You're sayin' you brought this fish to enter in the contest?"

I nodded.

"Got a New York State fishin' license?"

"I don't need one till I'm twelve."

"Is that right?"

"Yes, sir."

"Sure about that?"

"Yes, sir."

He looked at me. "Well, you're just one smart fella, aren't ya?"

I felt like I was going to cry but I didn't know why. The bass's tail flapped in the air.

He picked up the pen, clicked it. "So where's that mother of yours today?"

"She's waiting in the car," I said.

"Didn't feel like comin' in, huh?"

"No, it's just . . . she's not feeling well."

"That's too bad." He looked at the pad again, then flipped it closed. "Well—guess we better take a look." Getting off the stool, he strolled around the counter to where I stood by the bucket, looked at the fish, then slipped his fingers under its gill flap and lifted the great gleaming bulk into the air. I just stared at it. In the store it looked even bigger than it had on the lake. It was barely moving.

"Nice fish," he said. Carrying it dangling below his knee,

he walked back behind the counter, then lay it out on the brass bucket scale.

The bass lay still, only its gills opening and closing. I could hear him sliding the weights this way and that.

"Three pounds, fourteen ounces," he said. "Not bad—you're in second place."

I just looked at him. Every bass of that length I'd ever read about had weighed at least eight pounds.

"What?" he said.

I didn't say anything.

"Somethin' you want to say?"

I shook my head.

"Didn't think so."

He walked back around and put the fish back in the bucket for me, then said something about me coming back for plastic worms sometime. And I thanked him and I left.

MY MOM WAS hugging herself in her nightgown. How did it go? she said. She'd have given anything to see the look on his face.

I hoisted the bucket into the car. I didn't know I was going to do it. "It went great," I said, laughing. "You should've seen him—he could hardly talk."

She glanced at me quickly, then toward the entrance.

"I'm in second place," I said.

She hesitated for a long second, then smiled. "OK. Wow! That's great!"

We sat there for a few seconds, and then she started the car. I looked out the window while she bumped across the lot.

"My God, look at it," she said, almost to herself, as we waited at the road, and then: "Is it dead, you think?"

"Pretty sure," I said. I leaned forward to see. "Yeah."

"I just saw it breathe."

"That's just the water moving it around," I said.

"There it is again—look!"

Barely covered by water the huge gills opened, then closed, like a butterfly on a hot day.

We looked at each other.

"We can try," my mom said.

And we were off, back up 22, a hard right at the light, flying down the long, shady curves of Fairfield Drive.

"Is he still breathing?"

"I can't tell—I think so."

"Splash some water on him. Move him around a little."

She ran the stop sign at the war memorial. A car honked.

"Doesn't matter—is he still breathing?"

"I'm not sure."

"We're almost there."

And then we were back on the dirt road and the cabin was there and she was running for the camera while I lugged the bucket down through the tangled grass to the lake.

She took a picture but it didn't come out—I hadn't yet learned how to present myself to the world, how to make my accomplishments seem larger than they are—and then I was wading straight into the lake, carrying it in my arms like a child, rocking it forward and back to send water through the gills. It tilted sideways, helpless, the white of its belly shining against the dark water, its half-dollar-sized eye staring up at the clouds. When I looked up my mother was standing on the shore with her hands hiding her mouth.

I see her there still.

And I felt the muscles flinch, felt it right itself slowly on its axis, and then it swam off my palm and disappeared against the bottom of the lake.

Conception

THEIR PICTURE FELL OUT OF AGEE'S *A Death in the Family*, I swear, two days after my father died, and I could hear him laugh: "My God, God's an undergraduate. How about *No Exit*? Or Beckett's *Worstward Ho*?" I'd been packing boxes, drinking, my eyes as red as a rabbit's, when it slipped from between the loosened pages, cradled down, came to rest on my sock: Mom and Dad, half my age. Mom had been gone a while. Now he was too, and I was having a bit of trouble with that. How could you be— and then not?

In the picture they're in their bathing suits, looking up from Adirondack chairs submerged in the uncut grass. It's summer: that deep, grateful shade, tiny planes of light in the tall glasses— the ice cubes in their drinks haven't melted yet. I can see it in the way they're sitting, in the afternoon breeze blurring the zinnias behind my mother's left shoulder—this is before me. My father's just said something to the person with the camera; my mother, wearing a short terrycloth robe over her bathing suit, is looking down, smiling, like she can't help it. Like they've just had an argument and she's still angry but she can't help it. They look happy.

"The truth is, you almost weren't," my father said to me once. "The summer your mother and I got married there were some misunderstandings; we took a wrong turn and it kept getting worse." He smiled. "Hard to have a kid with somebody you're not talking to."

"So what happened?" I said.

"Who the hell knows?" he said.

HE'D WALK OVER to Elsa Durer's cabin the summer before I was born, I heard years later. It wasn't far to her place—you could see it from our dock: the roof and a bit of dusty window showing through the leaves, the air between quick with bugs that would show up as little corkscrews of light in old photographs.

I imagine her reading. She'd look up and see my father stepping over the poison ivy, his drink out for balance as if offering it to the trees, and wait until he'd walked into the curtain's edge, then put down her book and go out the back and down the stairs her husband had built after fifteen years of nagging. She could still see him kneeling in the wet grass with a cigarette in his mouth, sawing the cross planks. His strong, thin shoulders. When he'd nailed them to the two-by-fours that morning, a second hammer had answered from the far shore.

My father would be standing by her tree-slab table in the heat. "You know, it's worse when you move," he'd say.

"Then we better not move," she'd say.

"Reading?"

She'd sit in the wicker chair, light a cigarette. "The problem is, I really don't care who done it," she'd say, pushing the pack over to him. "You?"

He'd shake his head, sink into the other chair. "Christ. The air's like cotton."

"A heavy blanket."

"Oppressive."

"Stifling."

"When it moves, it's hot as an oven."

Lifting her head slightly and pushing out her lower lip she'd let out a thin wall of smoke. "You know, it's really not the heat, it's the humidity."

He'd smile, distracted, then reach for the pack. He looked like the actor Leslie Howard, she thought. That same air of confident uncertainty, that same troubled intelligence, like a slim knife in the brain.

SHE'D BE A good listener, the kind of woman who looks at you as you talk, her eyes moving slowly over your face. She'd be wearing a white summer dress, a small string of pearls. Her hair, still wet from the lake, would be pushed straight back, her legs bare. And they'd gossip about the neighbors, then meander from Dorothy Parker to party straws to the situation in Poland (the ice cubes all the while quietly clicking like miniature coconuts, shrinking into silence) until, suddenly frowning, he'd say, "I really should be getting back."

"Of course. It's getting late."

He'd sweep some imagined crumbs off the table, then stand, reluctantly. "So, anyway, you'll let us know if there's anything we can do."

"Don't forget your glass," she'd say, looking out over the lake. A hot breeze would move the leaves on her arms, her dress.

And that would be that, never mind the low light, the cicadas rising like a saw heard through a slowly opening window, her dampened hair—these only go so far. In 1958, you see, my father was thirty-one; Elsa Durer—already eleven years a widow— nearly eighty-two. So.

Still, when she died in November of 1969, my father went to the service on East Eighty-Third and York and sat there hunched forward, slowly rubbing his thumb over his knuckles. He'd called me to see if I'd come with him. When they were done I asked if he wanted to get something to eat. "It's OK," he said— then said it again.

He hadn't heard the question. He wasn't talking to me.

THE SUMMER THEY were married was hot, hotter than usual; he'd wake to the mosquitoes singing at the screen, and lie there, stupefied, trying to peel back the corner of the life he'd just had that he couldn't remember anymore. She'd still be asleep, as far from him as the bed would allow. He'd been alone, trying to explain something. Nobody was listening.

The week before, New York had hit 103, DC, 106. It was like something had broken: The water snakes by the dam, gorged on dying fish, withdrew into the stones like retractable cords, their keeled scales rasping against the rocks; the lake looked like the glass in the windows of cast-iron stoves.

He read. His wife read. They talked. *Would you like the front page? Some more coffee? Did you see the Lippmann piece?* So polite. When their friends drove up from Queens for the weekend they'd sit around the card table in their bathing suits like colorful toads and talk over each other and he'd remember the bottom of the community pool in Rego Park, he and his sister miming surprise, then laughter, waving to imaginary friends as the forest of legs around them pedaled endlessly on—he didn't know how long he could stand it.

They hadn't made love in weeks. It had been nothing—a suggestion. In bed, a few drinks down. Nothing.

He pretended it didn't matter, insisted—"Forget it, OK? Really. Just drop it."—then let himself feel aggrieved, wounded. When she pulled back, angry because he wouldn't talk to her, he let it run. After all, what did *he* have to apologize for? She was the one who'd made him feel ridiculous—let her come to him. She thought she knew him but she didn't. She didn't know him at all.

He glanced over the top of his newspaper now, wondering if she was really reading. Trapped in the oil-slick pools of her sunglasses, a bulbous head floated over a tiny body in a red bathing suit. Recognizing himself, he instinctively started to sit back to correct the image—then quickly leaned forward again. The hell with it. What did he care?

Sometimes, feeling like he was drowning, he'd go for a walk, carrying his drink through the overheated woods. And it really would make him feel better, just talking about Adlai Stevenson with someone who found him witty (and Stevenson too, for that matter), who didn't get that look, then cover her mouth with three fingers, who listened to him like he was actually *there*—until, that is, he'd notice the time and, trying not to seem like a tardy schoolboy jumping at the bell, stand—lazily, almost arrogantly—and with a last bit of wit, turn to go.

"Don't forget your glass," she'd say. She'd be looking out over the lake, not distracted, just listening the way old people will. And he'd wander back home past the water shadows wavering slowly up the trunks, the afternoon at a different pitch.

HE'D FIND HIS wife standing on the cool cement floor of the kitchen, stirring a tiny tornado into her drink. Or asleep in the hammock, frowning as if confused by something, her slim legs crossed at the ankles, a book roofed over her ribs. He'd walk up the path on the roots the runoff had laid bare and look at her, her right arm thrown back, her fingers knotted loosely through the ropes, then squat down on his heels and watch her sleeping. He'd look at her hair, her mouth, her breasts. Who was she, really? The question would make him uneasy. He could go. He could leave her. It was unthinkable—after four months his own voice sounded unfamiliar to him if she wasn't there to hear it—but he could. Maybe he would.

He'd lean closer, trespassing now. Where the sun had worked its way through the leaves, beads had sprung up on her cheek like oil in a pan.

He missed how she used to look at him. He missed how he used to love her.

She was right there. Nothing had changed.

Everything had changed. She found him ridiculous. Everything had changed.

A fly lit in her hair, glinted green. He waved it away.

SOMEBODY WAS PLAYING "Summertime" on a record player that summer, and he'd hear their voices coming over the still waters of the cove, ironic and magnificent: Ella's limpid control in the first verse, Satchmo's cat-scratch caress in the second, the two of them coming together in the third, the melody drawing the words—*Yer dad-dy's rich, and yer ma iiis good-lookin'*—down into the registers of regret. Ma was good-lookin' all right, he thought; Daddy, alas for him, far from rich.

But it wasn't that—though it might have become that in time. It wasn't about the money. Or the play he'd been writing that he couldn't write. It was what it always is: an inadvertent smile where passion was wanted, a moment's hesitation. A whispered shame, dared at last—*touch me, tell me, imagine him then*—returned by fear, desire too quickly exposed. And now it was too late. Real shame had flowered like rot. It would go underground, spread and grow like those ant colonies scientists say underlie entire counties. Love has died of lesser things.

Her attempts to set things right would seem crude, scripted, pathetic: the half-dropped towel, the brush of her breasts as she reached for the plates. So easily spurned. There was a power in not understanding, he'd find, in not seeing, in *not* taking her hips to move her aside in the kitchen but saying, instead, "Excuse me," then politely getting what he needed, ignoring her, winning. Hurting himself, but winning. *What?* he'd imagine saying, letting her suffer. *What? I needed to get to the sauce.*

It wouldn't take long—a time, maybe two. Pain trumps love. She'd be confused, then quickly defensive, hurt: *He'd taken her by surprise that night when he'd asked—he couldn't give her a moment to think? Fine, maybe she'd been a little embarrassed—he had to run off and sulk like a spoiled child, refusing to touch her, to see her attempts to make it right? She loved him. She hardly knew who he was anymore. So self-involved, so full of himself, unable to finish anything. And anyway, fuck Adlai Stevenson.*

They'd both be outside of it now, disbelieving, watching it unfold. Helpless. The original misunderstanding would fade into irrelevance; the cruelties it bred would fatten and thrive.

And then, heartbreakingly quickly, sickened by it, perhaps even welcoming its relief, they'd take the quick turn to hate.

AT THE BOTTOM of the summer, on a full moon, the whine of the mosquitoes sounding in his ears, he folded up the *Times*, stepped out of his shorts, and lifted the towel from the door. "Going for a swim," he said. "Mmm," she said, not looking up.

The moon, hidden by the oaks, had lit the opposite shore; he could see the stage lighting, the reflection of the tree line— a darker jade. The night was like warm skin, the water as he slipped off the dock and waded out, the same temperature as the air. Dimly, he felt the beauty of this, and then the pain over-whelmed him. There was no way out of this misery, no way back to where they'd been. He knew that now. He swam to the tree line's shadow, then out into the light, where he stopped.

He could feel the water moving between his legs, tight against his body.

He was swimming at an angle, twenty yards from her dock, when he heard something and stopped, treading water, unsure. Her cabin was dark. In the distance a bullfrog started; tentatively, another answered. Nothing. He'd begun to swim again when he heard it a second time, faint, breathless: "Please."

He swam toward the shore, listening. It seemed melodramatic, unbelievable—something out of a bad detective novel.

"Please. Is someone there?"

"Elsa?" This time it was clear. "It's me—I'm right here."

"Where?"

"In the lake."

"Please, I think I may have hurt something."

"Don't move," he said.

He felt the muddy bottom, scraped his foot on a rock, then scraped it again hurrying out on the shore. Under the trees, without his glasses, all he could see were a few streaks of faint light coming through the leaves and a kind of emptying which he knew would be the space around her cabin. He hurried toward it, ignoring the branches, one hand in front of his face like a bad actor turning away from something unpleasant, the other cupping his balls.

He could make out the bulk of the cabin now. "Where are you?" he whispered.

"Here, by the steps," she said, her voice pleading, close now. "I must have fallen. I was going for a swim and—Wait," she said, suddenly panicked, "I'm not wearing anything."

"Don't worry, I'm not either." It was out before he knew it—

absurd but effective. There was no time for that. And then he was there.

She was lying on the wooden steps, one arm extending languidly into the air as though she'd decided to lean back against them. Frightened. Humiliated. Crying, he thought. It occurred to him she might have hurt her spine. "Don't move," he said when she tried to sit up. "I'm here now. Can you feel your legs?"

She could. "How about your arms?" he said, as though he knew what the hell he was talking about. "Please, don't move— do you want me to call an ambulance?"

Even in the dark he could see the bewilderment in her face. She'd been afraid to stand up, she said. She'd been lying there, for hours it seemed, before she thought she heard someone out in the water. She'd tried to call out. She hadn't known what to do.

"It's OK, I'm here now." He was still squatting next to her. He could hear her breathing slowing—feel her coming back to herself. She didn't need an ambulance, she said.

"You sure?"

"I feel like such a fool."

"Don't be ridiculous," he said, shaken by the strange familiarity of her legs, by her slack, sunken belly, by her narrow, deflated breasts: "Anyone can fall."

"I think I'm all right now," she said, trying to sit up. "I think maybe I can—"

"Nonsense," he said, and ignoring her protests he slipped one arm under her back, another under her knees, and lifted her up. He was surprised by how little she weighed—relieved as well— and walking up the stairs, his back to the cabin for balance, her skin cool against his fingers, he pushed the door open with his foot, then kicked it gently shut behind him. Carrying her through the darkened cabin, he lay her on her bed, then pulled the sheet and covered her.

"Thank you," she said.

"You'll be all right?"

"I feel so ashamed."

He shook his head. "No," he said. And reaching out he brushed her thin hair back from her forehead, then a last strand, and left.

HE SWAM BACK along the wooded horizon of the moon, recalling her lying there across the steps. My God, what time could do. Would. The way the flesh of her thighs hung off the bone. Her arms. Her pelvis straining under the skin like the backs of the chairs his mother would use to prop up the tented rooms he'd play in for a while.

She was already asleep when he rolled her gently over in the dark, ignoring her arguments, her annoyance, her anger and surprise, saying, "I'm sorry, I'm sorry," then "shhhh, shhhh, it's OK, it's OK, it doesn't matter," holding her face in his hands, feeling her rising, answering, warily at first, then stronger and faster as the tears came on, whispering it over and over like an incantation, "I love you, I need you, shhhh, shhhh, it doesn't matter, it doesn't matter, it doesn't matter."

1963

He heard one chair creak, then the other. A game was on the radio. "I've got to work on that piece today," he heard his father say. "Good for you," said Mr. Hauser's voice. "Really," his father said.

"Los Angeles Angels—dumb name for a baseball team," said Mr. Hauser.

"Maybe they think it'll bring them luck," said his father.

A burst of laughter came from the float on the lake, which he could see through a crack in the wallboards. A half dozen people—marked, like croquet poles, by the horizontal stripes on their bathing suits—milled about, some settling into folding chairs, others standing around with drinks in their hands.

"How long you think before one of 'em falls in?"

"Weissman in ten," said his father.

It was very hot. A small spider had built a web between the frame of the bed and the metal leg. The web was spotted with gnats. The spider seemed to be sleeping. He blew on it but it didn't move. A dusty pencil with a broken tip was lying by the wall and he picked it up and poked a hole in the web like a small dark window, then moved the pencil in a circle to make the hole bigger and the spider ran across the web and then back again.

"Is she out there?" said Mr. Hauser's voice.

"No."

"What about him?" Mr. Hauser said.

"The kid? Not likely."

"If I was Leventis, I'd shoot him."

"No, you wouldn't."

"I'd think about shooting him, then."

They were quiet for a moment.

"Where is everybody?" said Mr. Hauser.

"Mary's out at the A&P. I don't know where Harold is. Fishing, I think."

It was hot under the bed. When Harold turned his head to the side a little, he could see watery shapes moving slowly up the walls. It felt funny to hear his father call his mother by her name.

"Another?" his father said.

"What the hell."

"I think he wants to surprise me."

"Who?"

"Harold," his father said. Through the open door he could see his father's white, hairy feet in their sandals walk across the floor. He tried not to laugh.

"So what do you think he'll do?"

"Who? Leventis?" His father was in the kitchen. "He'll either leave her or he won't."

"What's to stay for?" said Mr. Hauser. A cicada started its

long, uphill climb. "Still, I guess you can see it from the little punk's point of view. I mean, look at her."

His father laughed. "A minute ago you were gonna shoot him."

"*Him*, not me. Anyway, tell me you'd push her little boat away if she rowed up to your rickety dock one night while Mary was out at the A&P."

"I'm not going to tell you that," his father said from the kitchen. He could hear ice cubes dropping into a glass. "So is that a metaphor—rickety dock?"

"It's a misstrike."

"Ah."

"Something to think about, you have to admit," said Mr. Hauser.

"Her little boat? Oh, I think we've all thought about it."

He heard his father spin the metal cap back on, then the clink of the bottles touching under the sink. He thought about coming out—he was tired of being under the bed—but didn't.

He heard his father walk to the screen door and then the spring made a stretching sound and the door banged twice against the frame and his father said, "We don't have to worry about malaria anymore," and Mr. Hauser said, "Thank God for that," and the chair creaked.

"Christ, it's Leventis," he heard his father say.

"Jesus. What's he doing?"

"Bailing his boat it looks like. By his rickety dock."

He heard Mr. Hauser lean forward in the wicker chair. "I don't see her."

"He's going out alone. Just ignore it, they have a nest somewhere under the eave."

"How the hell am I supposed to ignore a wasp when it's crawling on my glass?"

"Funny, I never liked him much," his father said.

"You think he couldn't talk her into coming out?"

"My guess is he's just putting one foot in front of the other."

"I'll never understand that."

"Nothing to understand. He's in love with his wife."

Mr. Hauser laughed. Far away, the people on the float burst into laughter, as if they had heard the joke too. It was hot. Something about the sound made him feel sleepy.

"Love," said Mr. Hauser, as though he didn't like the word.

"Close, anyway."

"She's screwing some kid."

"Doesn't always go away when you want it to."

"Love? Goddammit, now what do I do? I thought you said if I ignored it, it wouldn't happen."

"Just flip it out with the fork."

"I should let it drown."

"So let it drown. Look, I'm just saying that . . ."

He tried to listen but he was very sleepy. The spider was sitting, perfectly still, over the pencil hole in the web, as if thinking about it. For a moment he felt bad about having made the hole; then he picked up the pencil and put it back in the hole and moved it around until the hole was the size of a quarter. He was very sleepy.

"—NOT A COMPLETE idiot," Mr. Hauser was saying. "I know it's not all *The Book of Man* or whatever."

"What book of man?" his father said.

"You know, that Steichen book everybody was going on about a couple of years ago. All those happy couples with manure shovels, or holding each other in the grass . . . Molly Bloom and all that shit."

"I liked that book."

"I'm saying I know it's never that simple, but . . ."

From far away came a yelp and a rising chorus of yells, as if someone were being thrown up in a blanket, followed by a big splash.

"Take a look," said his father.

Mr. Hauser laughed. "Weissman." He could tell by the way his voice changed that Mr. Hauser was looking through the binoculars.

"Not even noon and he's potted like a plant."

"So what's he doing?"

"Who? Leventis? Just sitting there. Smiling like he's been shot."

The chair creaked. Again his father's feet walked to the kitchen. "Whoa, slow down, Captain," said Mr. Hauser. Again he heard the cap, the clink of the bottles. They sounded far away. He wondered when his mother would be back. His father's feet returned to the porch.

"Where were we?" said Mr. Hauser.

"You were explaining how life isn't always like Edward Steichen."

"Sometimes, I said."

"Sometimes not like Edward Steichen." His father burped. "Let me tell you something: Life is never like Edward Steichen."

"Fine."

"Because it doesn't stop, it doesn't strike a pose and grow a frame, it just . . . crawls on."

"Christ, have another drink."

"Let me tell you a little story—"

"Jesus, here we go . . ."

"It's about how life isn't always like Edward Steichen. I have this friend, about my age, happily married . . . One kid—a girl."

"Happily married, one girl. Got it."

"So three years ago he's flying home from Atlanta and he ends up sitting next to this young thing with perfumed breasts like Molly fucking Bloom and they end up talking all the way to LaGuardia. She hangs on his every word, laughs at his jokes. They have their little tables down and he can feel her thigh pressed up against his. When they get in it's dark and she offers him a ride—she's got a car right there and it turns out they live near each other—and on the way she says she has to make a stop at her office. The place has a great view, she says, it'll only take a minute, and since he feels like an idiot saying he'll just wait in the car like he's afraid of her—he's spent the last two hours talking about his wife like he's building a dam—he goes up with her and the place is huge and dark except for the lights from the city and feels like high school used to feel the night of a play. Like something could happen. Like the usual rules don't apply."

"Uh-oh."

"It's making him sweat. He's following her around in the dark like a goddamn cocker spaniel, admiring the view, then her desk, then her coworker's desk, and all the time what he wants to say is that he really has to go, that it's getting late—he can actually *see* his wife waiting up for him, the kid asleep upstairs, even realizes in some far-off way that if this goes where it's going there's no coming back—but then she kind of leans against a doorframe so he can look inside an office and he brushes by her and suddenly he's got her breasts in his hands and anyway they do it twice on the carpet between the desks—matching knee burns, the whole thing."

"Good story."

"You haven't heard the best part yet. The twist is that even before our hero's put his dick back in his pants he realizes that next to his kid the thing he valued most in this world was that he'd never had to lie to his wife, that he could be exactly who he was, that all their shit was out in the open, and that he's taken this thing and thrown it off some high rise on Fifty-Seventh Street. He feels like he did the day his father died. Like something's gone. Like it doesn't even matter if his wife ever finds out, because *he'll* know."

"I'd have to say he should have thought about that before. So what happens?"

"Pretty much what you'd expect happens. The girl calls, the wife gets suspicious—doesn't matter. Anyway, it all comes out."

"And the wife leaves him?"

"That's twist number two—she stays. You see, they both love their kid to distraction—the thought of telling him, you know, you'll see Daddy every other Saturday is not something they can do, so they just go on."

"So she forgives him."

"Not about forgiveness. It's been three years. Everything looks fine from the outside, but they're like, I don't know, like a bone that's healed crooked."

"He should give it time."

"Good idea."

"I mean it. Tell him if he loves her . . ."

"Maybe he should get her a copy of *The Family of Man*."

"If he loves her . . ."

"Don't you get it? Love's the problem. He's given her all this pain and now he's starting to hate her for it."

"Listen to me. He'll be all right. He's just in the middle of this thing, so he can't see, but . . ."

"Maybe he can be like that guy in the paper with the bullet in his head. Learn to live with it. Stay away from magnets."

"All I'm sayin' is . . . What the hell was that?"

When they found him under the bed, he was sound asleep.

"Here's your surprise."

"Christ, I thought he was out fishing."

"How long you think he's been here?"

"Too long."

"So let him sleep. Maybe he didn't hear."

When he woke, his father and Mr. Hauser were still talking on the porch. The Angels didn't have a prayer, Mr. Hauser was saying.

He looked at the web. A single strand, like a tightrope walker's line, stretched across the dark window, cutting it almost in half.

Dog

THE FIRST TIME IT HAPPENED HE THOUGHT a hornet had crawled into her fur—it was a cold, lowering day in October—or that she'd lodged a shard of glass in her hair while rolling in the dirt. They had been sitting above the dam, her knobby, buried spine pressed against his thigh, and when he yelled and leaped to his feet she lurched up with a startled bark to attack whatever it was that had frightened him. He looked at his hand: a miniature red-walled crevasse had opened into the second joint of his index finger; in the instant before the startled blood rushed in, he could see down into his flesh.

His first responsibility, of course, was to reassure her, and so, clamping the cut between his thumb and ring finger, he gently called her over. She came right away, relieved and apologetic. "Come here, baby," he said, "let's take a look at what's goin' on in there." He'd been pulling on her ears, he remembered, feeling the fuzzy whorls of cartilage on the underside with his thumb, but when he looked there was nothing there. She whined, restless, beseeching. "Shhh, hold still," he said.

He found it in the thick ruff of hair at the base of her skull: a thin, gunmetal sliver of steel rising perhaps an inch above the stippled skin like a rectangular fin. It made no sense. Was it glued on, somehow? Spreading back the coarse fur he flipped the thing gently back and forth with the pinky of his hurt hand and felt his throat clutch with nausea: it was buried in the skin, the thick flange of the base half-submerged beneath the surface. Taking off his glasses he could read the make—True Test—inscribed in the steel, the bottoms of the letters rising out of the plain. There was no way around it; it was what it was.

For a moment, pity overwhelmed him and the yellow leaves and the dark brushstrokes of trunks along the far shore softened and blurred. He loved her: her big, foolish, loyal eyes, her solidity and strength. How many times had he woken to a groaning board, an up-sliding sash, and been glad to know that she was there, vigilant, terrifying to anyone who might wish him harm.

The air moved and she looked up, her spongy, big-pored nose twitching as if invisible flies were settling on it. How can you itemize love? He remembered bringing her home from the pound in a towel-lined carton that had once held twelve cans of Campbell's Split Pea Soup. He loved her long English face, her tongue, smooth as veal, the late-October smell of her fur. They'd watch TV together. They'd lie next to each other on the rug and he'd hear that deep, shuddering, contented sigh, and sliding down to sleep on the trough and crest of her breathing he'd know that this was love, love as profound and true as the slowing of blood when the season's screw starts to tighten.

And now something, or someone, had tried to hurt her. Had hurt her. Had embedded this thing—but how was this possible?—in her flesh. He wanted to grab it with his fingers, rip it from her skin. Make her who she'd been. "I'm sorry, baby," he whispered, "I'm sorry." She whined happily, hearing his voice. He forced himself to look again. There were no sutures, no signs of trauma; her skin where it bulged like a low dune over the flared base of the blade was wax-smooth, as if grown to the steel. When he stood, a kingfisher threw itself across the pond, trailing its rapid chattering cackle. It was time to go home, where they could put this bizarre incident behind them. When he touched her back, he cut himself again.

The next morning, under the bright light of the reading lamp, he found four more, and a deep shudder of shame ran through him. How could this have happened? Something had to be done, and soon, before it went any further. Carrying the floppy brick of the phone book over to the table with his good hand, he phoned Dr. Wilson's office and made an appointment for that afternoon. For some reason he felt nervous, and when the receptionist inquired after the nature of the problem, he answered, vaguely, that it was just a skin condition, and that he'd been hoping somebody could take a look at it. "It's probably nothing," he added nonsensically. A tickle of sweat rolled down his side. "And how long would you say she's had this condition, sir?" the receptionist asked. "Oh, not long . . . a few days," he answered. He didn't care for her tone.

An hour later, too agitated to sit down, he called back to say he'd have to reschedule at some other time. It was impossible. How could he bring her to Wilson's office with fifteen razor

blades—there were more by now—embedded in her skin?
They'd think he was responsible. He'd denied it—said it was
nothing. No, they'd be sure to blame him—and for good reason. Worse, they might think his sweet, sad-eyed girl was dan-
gerous; might want her put away somewhere, put down. It was
unthinkable.

Standing by the phone, unsure of what to do, he felt a tug at
his pants. Sensing his anxiety, she'd brushed against his leg, and
a new blade, protruding from between her poor ribs like the pec-
toral fin on a fish or the horizontal knife on a chariot's wheel, had
cut a neat one-inch slice through his pants just below his knee,
barely missing his skin. She was sitting on the carpet at his feet,
whining for forgiveness. He started to reach for her offered paw,
then patted the ridge above her nose instead. "It's OK, baby," he
said, "it's OK. I know you didn't mean it." She seemed mollified.
Her black mushroom nose twitched; her long pink tongue flowed
over her teeth. She loved him. "We'll have to lay low," he whispered to her, still petting her nose with his good hand, "we'll
have to keep this between us," and bathed in his voice she began
to wriggle with excitement, her hindquarters fishtailing to the
side like a tractor-trailer about to crash.

THE TWO OF them settled into a cripple's routine, improvised at
first, soon hardened into habit. There was even some beauty to
it—the two of them together, under siege. Late at night they'd
walk up to the elementary school, the short, frost-baked grass
caving under their feet, his breath pushing quill-less feathers
into the air. On certain nights it seemed like their shadows were

the last ones on Earth, like they could walk for years, unfolding the land—the valleys and hills and deserted little houses—
and all would sleep before them and the night would never end.
When they ran into neighbors, themselves out for a late walk,
he'd pretend to be colder than he was, hugging himself in his old
army jacket, and they'd hurry on. It couldn't be helped. After
a moment's inattention had opened a deep cut in his palm that
required stitches (he'd explained that he worked with glass) he'd
taken to wearing his heavy, mustard-yellow work gloves. People
might notice, and wonder.

It was possible, he thought, that it would pass; that all they
had to do was endure it as best they could, and all would be well.
It was even possible that the situation, difficult as it was, might
actually bring them closer. Certainly there were times, breaks
in the pain, when he realized again—as though he needed
reminding—that she was not the enemy, that it was the two of
them against this thing inside her, that in fact there was something regal about her suffering, something noble in her battle
with herself. She bore her trial with a dignity bordering on dis-
dain, walking next to him with the clusters of blades rustling and
clicking like a colony of mechanical insects; it moved him deeply.
If she hurt, she seemed to be saying, she hurt only for him; his
pain alone weighed in the balance.

Of course he couldn't deny that this was literally true as well:
she felt no pain. He'd tested this to put his mind at ease. One
evening, hearing her sigh and settle herself on her foam-filled
bed (the blades, with one or two exceptions, ran largely along
the ridge of her back), he called her over to the kitchen table. She
came immediately. "Good girl," he said, "that's my good girl."

She looked up, trusting him. "We're going to try something here," he said. "If it hurts, you just say so, OK?" She wagged her tail.

Pulling on his work gloves he cradled her head in one hand and with the other felt for a cluster of blades. Just above her left shoulder he found a group of four, tightly layered, leaning slightly like small steel playing cards. Propping them up to the perpendicular, he gently pressed down with his glove. Nothing. He pushed harder, drawing down the surrounding hair like trees growing from the side of a hill. When she wagged her tail, relief flooded his heart. Just as he'd hoped, the blades, like the spines on a porcupine, only cut one way. Whatever damage she might do to things outside, she herself felt little or nothing. For this he was grateful.

As the weeks passed there were moments, admittedly, when gratitude did not come easily, when self-pity and, yes, even anger rose up inside him. It wasn't just the unavoidable accidents that occurred despite all the precautions he'd taken—the gloves, the boots, even the rider's chaps he'd bought, feeling like a fool, at a horseback-riding supply store—it was her inability (or unwillingness) to understand, her insistence on seeing his attempts to protect himself as a kind of betrayal. His resentment shamed him. She loved him. Pet me, hold me, she seemed to say to him. Scratch my chest with your fingernails, bury your face in the folds of my neck. And there were times, looking into her eyes, so disappointed in him, so full of pain, when he wanted to.

There was nothing he could do. She lived for him. How could he say to her that love had its limits? He looked at her, sleeping peacefully on her bed. Three nights earlier, he'd fallen asleep in front of the television still wearing his boots and chaps and huge leather gloves like some middle-aged wrangler home from the range. Drugged by fatigue and worry, buried under the oceanic wash of voices and laughter, he didn't hear her when she awoke with a long, reedy yawn, rose, shook herself—her coat rattling and clashing like metal leaves in a sudden wind—and jumped on the couch to sleep by his side. He woke screaming, a four-bladed harrow digging into his ribs, staggered to his feet, and crashed over the coffee table. Still on his hands and knees like a man imitating a small horse waiting to be mounted, he felt her warm, flat tongue on his face. The pain in her eyes was like the touch of fire.

THANKSGIVING WAS A trial. Under the circumstances, there was no question of inviting friends, and so, reluctantly, he cut his usual recipe for cornbread stuffing by three-fourths and set to work. It wasn't easy. He moved with difficulty, what with the butterfly stitches on his hands and hip and the sutures on his ribs (he made the mistake of reaching for a can of corn in the pantry), but he managed. It was important to preserve some measure of normalcy, to allow himself a touch of happiness—after all, he'd done nothing to deserve this—but the guilt he felt putting her in the wooden crate in the living room leached all the joy from the evening. He crumbled the hard-boiled egg, awkwardly diced the celery and the green pepper, holding the butcher knife with his two good fingers, even tried to hum along with the music he'd put on, pathetically, then put everything in the refrigerator and went to bed.

He woke to a long hiss, as if someone were trying to get his attention. Hurrying down the stairs as best he could (the hip always stiffened in the night, and the painkillers made him dizzy) he turned on the light to the living room. It was as though some-one had tried to slice away the bottom of the room: a long, knee-high cut ran along the armoire and across the spines of books on the second shelves; the drapes had been sliced short; the soft white entrails of the couch and the loveseat and the leather chair bulged from their cushions. His first thought was that an intruder had been searching for something buried in the pillows or hidden behind the wallpaper sagging down like flayed flesh, and that she hadn't barked because something had happened to her. Then he heard her claws on the kitchen floor.

Relieved, he started toward her, limping quickly down the long hall. The claws stopped—she'd heard him, he realized—then began again, raining down on the linoleum as she rushed to meet him. Inexplicably (perhaps it was the rind of some forgotten dream) it seemed to him that in her changed state she might think he was the intruder; that at that very moment she was, in fact, coming after him. The same instant she appeared at the far end of the hallway, slipping slightly into the wall, a clattering, click-ing, long-tongued thing, overcome with love for him, and he saw that it didn't matter whether she was coming in love or fury, and genuinely terrified now, screaming at her to stop, he knocked the telephone table into her path, then brought the claw-footed base of the coatrack down on her head.

He didn't know he could bear that much pain. She lay on her side, her hind legs tangled in the telephone cord, her brown eyes looking at him from between the blades now growing out of her cheeks, her brows, with a kind of oceanic calm, an understanding and a forgiveness of this betrayal that shamed him to the core. Barely feeling the pain in his ribs, his hands, he crawled up and kneeled before her big, bristling head and wept. He could see the blood welling up almost directly between her ears, and though he didn't have his gloves, he managed to part the blades with his fingers, pushing down on their flat, smooth sides, and expose the gash. He could see her breathing, the blades arranging and rearranging themselves like scales. She was looking at him. "I'm sorry," he whispered, "I'm sorry," and reaching out he touched the small space on the bridge of her nose where the fur was still visible, then touched it again. Something cut him but he didn't stop. Her tail began to beat.

IT WASN'T HIM who first thought of doing it before the season turned the ground to stone, who limped up through the gap in the wall and into the stony pasture with a shovel and a six-foot crowbar and began what he couldn't conceive of beginning. The pasture that afternoon, so near the dam where they'd sat together only two months earlier, was full of thin November light, like watery cream. He'd never dug a grave before.

It wasn't hard. The shovel's blade slipped into the earth as easily as if the groove had been waiting for it; the big, brown rocks, which he pried from their perfect homes in the dirt and rolled, helpless, onto the leaves of the forest floor, offered little resistance. Looking up from his labors he could see the crimped tin of the lake through the trees. It wasn't him. He was on a plane, reading an article about a man digging a grave in a pasture; the wind coming off the lake was chilling the sweat on this man—someone he'd known, once.

He knew he didn't deserve this distance, and it didn't last long. The ease with which the ground opened up before him— that straight-sided rectangle deepening into its own shadow— made him sick with self-loathing. She would attack death itself for him, and yet here she was, tied to a small tree by the chain he'd had to substitute for the leather leashes she'd shredded to strips. He could see it in her face: she hated him now, and for forcing this last, deepest pain on her, she hated him more. She couldn't understand why he'd abandoned her, why he no longer loved her. The situation—the injustice and the cruelty of it, his helplessness in the face of it—made him frantic, and to punish himself he began to work with a kind of righteous violence, relishing the fire in his ribs as his due, twisting like a discus thrower to heave a thirty-pound rock out of the grave with a joyous grunt that sounded like a sob, tearing at the red roots with his hands until, feeling the warmth in his gloves, he pulled them off with his teeth, exposing the gaping little mouths of his cuts to the wind. He deserved no less.

There was nothing outside of them now. The grave, covered with a tarp and weighed down by rocks, remained where he left it. They returned home. He barely recognized her now, her once-familiar body a mass of blades that seemed to multiply daily, to fatten on his shame. Only her eyes remained unchanged, calm as the black little twigs under ice, watching him through the blade-gnawed bars of her crate. There was nothing to be done.

It came on the day of the season's first snow, a powdering that called attention to the edges of eaves and the crossbars of gates and fences and was gone by noon. They were on their way out. She had been waiting patiently while he searched his pockets for house keys, her chain clipped to her wire collar. Raising her leg to scratch at her side, she gave a startled yelp, and thinking she was being attacked, instantly bit her own rump. Unable to help her, her every cry like a fishhook in his throat, he watched her spin and crash through the house—a clattering, snarling dervish—until she'd worked herself into a corner by the couch, where he wrestled her down under her thick foam bed. He could feel her beneath him, whimpering and growling, and even as he yelled her name, frantically trying to break the spell, she worked her bloodied head free and sank her teeth in his arm.

It was nearly dusk. He'd wrapped her in a half dozen gray movers' blankets, and when he bent over the backseat to pick her up, he was surprised how light she'd grown. He lay her down on the leaves. As he moved the stones off the tarp, he could feel her eyes following him. The grave was as he'd left it, waist deep and perfect. "It's not my fault," he said aloud to himself. "It's not my fault."

The pills were from Mexico, a bright canary yellow. He gave her three in a piece of hamburger meat he'd brought in a plastic bag. He was already weeping when she began to lick his bleeding hand, working her warm tongue between his fingers. He couldn't do this, he thought.

But he did. Letting her lick the grease off his hand with her cut tongue, he jumped down into the grave and lifted her in his arms. There was plenty of room. Lying down beside her he drew one of the blankets partly over himself and looked up at the rectangle of branches and sky. He'd taken eight himself; there was nothing else to do. He could feel her against him, the slowing bellows of the lungs, the shallowing crest and trough. He looked over at her. Lying on her side, gravity pulling the lower gum back from her teeth, her tongue lolling, she seemed to be smiling.

Three brown leaves came over the rim. "Good dog," he said. "Good dog."

Half-Life

THERE'S A PLACE PAST BREATHING, discovered by deep-sea divers who swim ten stories down on a lungful of air. Past the pain. If you ignore the body's screaming, call its bluff, you enter a plain of stillness and light: the heart's tantrum passes, the lungs take back their shape. You swim on. Unlikely things begin to appear, serene and irrefutable. Eventually, according to those who have lived, dragged to the surface with ropes, you begin to laugh, which means you're finally dying.

A month ago I walked into the living room just in time to see my house go by on the evening news. I recognized it right away: the mossy awning, the garage, the small black window behind which I stood, watching my house go by on the news, and then it was gone. I hadn't seen it in sixteen years.

For a moment I felt something move, like in a dream when you can hear things—other things—through it. I changed the channel. Young people in torn clothing were turning something on a spit. A fat woman wept. A judge pounded his gavel. I kept switching. When the electricity went out, I sat in the dark and ate. Every few seconds the world lit up—a soft flash, no thunder. I could see everything: the bureau, the entrance to the kitchen, the plate on my lap. It began to rain.

IT'S NOT WHAT you think. I'm not like the ones you find sitting on piles of filthy bedding after a rowhouse fire in Memphis. I've kept myself in good health. I swim in my pool after dark. I don't smell of cat urine. I just prefer my own company. It's not unreasonable, really. I live in Florida. Ten minutes away, unless it's moved, is the bus stop where Ratzo Rizzo came to die.

Things happen the way they do, or did. My mother and father immigrated from Berlin not long after the war—nothing sinister; father was in air-conditioning, so . . . Florida. Now I'm the one in air-conditioning. When they died—so long ago now I can't see their faces—I moved into the house with my husband, Stanislav, where we lived together, happily shaking the dew from our days until one night he rolled off me and said, "I can't do this." He was looking up at the ceiling as if reading a message someone had written there. "I'm seeing someone," he read, and I said, "Seeing?" and he sighed and said, "Fine, I'm fucking someone, I'm in love with someone," and that, as they say, was that.

Did I love him? Maybe I did. It doesn't matter. I took it badly, I'm not sure why, exactly. People are like bones—they break differently.

I stayed on after he left. The world felt loose to me suddenly, like a table you can't quite lean on. Eventually I grew used to things, like everyone does. It's our great strength—no outrage on earth we can't make our own. And that's it. The mail comes, the mail goes. I have the food delivered to a small refrigerator on the front porch. I pay the bills. I've been blessed with quality appliances; repairmen come rarely.

Do I ever wish that things might have been otherwise? I'm sixty-two years old—I've made my bed. I prefer it, given the choices. And anyway, it comes to the same thing: either way it ends, and sooner than we'd like. The half-life of love is not that long.

I CAN TELL you this: aloneness does things. Your face in the mirror becomes her face too. The furniture comes out of its shell. After a year the bureau, the vanity, the worn chair in which you eat your meals, all have a point of view. After two, they can make you angry. Dreams flare, then die. You want to be still. To be left alone. To not have to move until you don't have to. I know how it sounds, but trust me—there's some peace in this.

All of which explains why these things happening to me lately have affected me the way they have, why the sight of my house on T V, for example, gliding by as if on a conveyer belt, troubled me as much as it did. You get sensitive—I won't deny it. When you've spent sixteen years looking out, you don't want to think about looking in. When you're sitting alone in a room, a room you've spent sixteen years emptying of everything until it roars like a shell, the sound of someone clearing their throat can stop your heart.

It's reasonable enough. You make your place, draw your line. It should be your choice, who crosses over, who doesn't.

Two weeks ago I dropped my glasses behind the couch,

but when I tried to pull the couch out from the wall, it wouldn't move. It seemed stuck on something. There were no nails. I checked the rug to see if it was in the way, then tried again. Nothing. A slight tearing sound. I went into the kitchen for a flashlight. At first I couldn't understand what I was looking at: there was some kind of cord wrapped around the hind legs; the undersides of the cushions had sprouted leaves.

I cut the legs free with a knife and a pair of pliers, but even afterward, with the couch lying on its back in the middle of the room and the vine in pieces on the rug, I couldn't understand what it could have wanted. It had come through a crack in the wall, pried its way deep into the springs and cushions. I kept pulling and pulling, sickened by the sound of ripping from inside. A pencil-thin shoot, as strong as twine, had crawled around the back of the bookshelf; when I pulled on it, the shelf began to tip forward. I followed it up to a hole in the backboard. Behind the top row of books I found a wiry little nest, like hair.

It wasn't so unreasonable; strange, yes, but not unreasonable. This was Florida. All sorts of things grow in this climate. Over the next few days I pulled the couch out, reassured every time it slid across the floor, to check the spot where I'd sawed the vine flat to the wall. It looked like the scar after a mole is removed. It seemed dead. To make sure, I forced it back out with the tip of a screwdriver, then covered the crack with duct tape. I didn't think about it again until the evangelist came.

USUALLY I'D SEE them coming up the drive, wiping their faces with their handkerchiefs, and just go into the bedroom until they left. They never lasted long. For some reason they'd always come by around midday, and it's hot as the sun on the porch at midday.

This time I just looked up and there he was at the window, looking at me. I couldn't move. There was something grotesque about him, something slack and distended, as though he'd been bigger once and some air had been let out. He just stood there, staring at me. I couldn't move. I could feel my blood thickening like tar, filling up my throat. And then he stuck out his tongue, licked two fingers, and began to rub something on his cheekbone. Turning his head to the side he rubbed some more, then wiped his face with his tie.

I don't know what it was—relief, maybe—but at that moment I felt a short, sharp spasm, vague as memory. I could see the sweat trickling down his face and neck. It must have been some quirk in the glass: When he looked at me, all he could see was himself looking in, or the books behind my chair. I began to wonder how long he'd last, and why he'd bother. Had he heard something? At some point he took a coin out of his pocket and tapped it on the glass and I could see the wet matted hair on his arm.

He held on longer than I thought. When he finally stepped back and glanced up at the roof as if he might find me sitting there, then threw his jacket over his shoulder and walked away, I felt sick to my stomach.

By the time the hurricane came, I'd started dreaming again—just remnants, nothing I could hold. I hadn't asked for it. The men from the grocery store sank everything the wind could take in the pool, then nailed the boards over the windows, quickly dimming the house into dusk—and left. That night I watched Abel coming on TV—the heavy, swinging traffic lights, the horizontal rain, the young newscaster leaning into the wind, his clothes trapped against his body like birds against a fence—then sat in the dark when the electricity went out and listened to the wind screaming, the rolling, hammering sound of things torn loose . . . The night before I'd dreamt I was in a house crammed with tables and dressers and doors, leaning against each other like cards, and as I walked down a dark hallway lined with rooms like a train going by at night I saw my father sitting in a wing-back chair, staring at the place I'd just walked through.

I WANT TO be very calm, very precise when I say this. The day after Abel left the men came and took the boards off the windows. The rain had stopped but the wind still gusted up now and then, shaking the palms, turning the puddles to iron, then back. By evening it was dead and beautiful, every point dripping water, huge, man-of-war-purple clouds growing to the west. I went out after dark, as I always do, to take out of the pool whatever had fallen into it. There wasn't much—a few palmetto bugs, one of those splinter-thin lizards that nod and jerk in the shrubbery, a small white moth . . . I scooped them up carefully so they wouldn't come apart and walked out the screen door. As I threw them into the dark I noticed a round depression in the soaking grass just inside the light, as if a statue had recently stood there, and realized I was looking at a cat print the size of a plate. I just stood there, holding the frying pan spatter guard I've used ever since a guinea pig broke my net. Then I started to shake.

I remember thinking it might be a joke—some kid with a plastic tiger paw on a stick. It was what it was. There was a ridge, like a miniature cliff, where the weight had pressed the upper part of the heel into the dirt. I ran my finger over it. I had to. Then I walked to the house and turned on the outer light and there it was, another one, harder to make out, because the grass was better there, but as real as anything between heaven and earth. I looked around. Nothing moved. For just a moment, I wanted to laugh. I could see the ovals of the claw pads, the triangle of the heel. Then, only a few feet from the hedge, I found a hairy pile of stuff specked with bits of bone, and knew. You could imagine tracks, I thought. Nobody imagines shit. I went back inside.

I knew what it was, of course. It had happened before; a hurricane had come through, some animals had broken out of their enclosures . . . I started watching the news to see if one of the big cats had escaped from the zoo, but there was nothing, and then it occurred to me that if something had actually gotten out, they might try to get it back inside quietly to avoid a panic. It seemed plausible.

All the next day I kept expecting to see something, police cars, men with nets, the sound of helicopters beating the air—nothing. I couldn't explain it. By late afternoon I'd started to doubt myself, as anyone would, so I went out again—in the daylight this time. The tracks were just where I'd left them, along with new ones from the night before. I could see it perfectly. I could see where he'd come over the fence, unstoppable, where the huge front paws had touched down. The neighbor's irritating little dog, I noticed, was not on its chain. Sure enough, when I looked I could see where he'd stopped the night before, suddenly sensing the dog on its chain, where he'd moved along the fence, trying to find an opening, where he'd pivoted, gathered and leaped—here were the big stripes of dirt where the claws had dug in—effortlessly clearing the fence, the hedge, the shrubs . . .

There was nothing else to do. To try to sleep would have been insane, truly. I was sixty-two years old. When would I ever have a chance like this again? I wanted to see him. I pulled a couch under the big screen window over the pool. I worried for a while about what to wear—something dark seemed the obvious choice, but the couch itself was almost white. I finally decided on a dark top, which wouldn't show against the wall, and a light pair of slacks. I ate a small dinner, then went out to the veranda, into the heat, and arranged the cushions. It had started to rain again. You could hear it here, outside the air-conditioning, pounding on the tin roof. I knelt on the couch, my arms on the sill. It was quite dark. Now and then I could feel something small and tight move in my chest.

He came an hour or two after midnight, an unbelievable thing. One moment there was just the spellbound yard, still as death, the next he was there, touching down, right foot, then left, soft as a cloud, mountainous. I'd never seen anything like him. I never will again. He didn't move so much as flow over the ground, his huge head down between his shoulders . . . I could see the stripes, sinuous as smoke—he seemed boundless, uncontainable.

I watched him sniff like a dog at the rusted sink that my father had put out by the fence, then move in a heavy, gliding trot to the outside screen. There was something presumptuous about the way he went from spot to spot, disdainful, methodical; he was looking for something. At the corner of the screened enclosure, a few feet from the door, he abruptly stopped short and I felt my bladder give a little. He'd smelled me, I thought. For a long time—ten seconds, maybe more—he didn't move; then, slightly raising his powerful hindquarters, he gave a kind of convulsive jerk, then another and I heard the thick, obscene jets hitting the stones of the patio. Finished, he walked to the strip of grass between the screen and the fence and settled himself on the ground, haunches first. My God he was beautiful. He lay on his side for a while looking over the grass, then turned on his back, and was still. An hour passed. At times I could barely make him out—just a huge black shape against the grass. He seemed to fill the yard.

The next thing I knew he was up and pawing at the screen door to the pool. He got a claw in and the door swung open. For the first time I began to be afraid. I was kneeling, completely unprotected, on a sofa behind a screen. I couldn't draw a full breath. My thighs were jerking uncontrollably. I watched him walk to the pool past the deck chair, past the place with the missing tiles, the pile of rotten carpets. He was right there. I could see the muscles in his legs, his billiard-sized balls swinging in their velvet sack. He stopped, listening, then dipped his huge head to the water. He was so close now I could hear the soft slap of his tongue touching the roof of his mouth.

I didn't move. I couldn't move. I watched him drink, then wade slowly into the warm water at the shallow end, only his head and shoulders showing above the water. The window, the screen, were nothing. I knew that. These things were like air to him.

And then he looked up from the water and rose in a great, ripping gush and suddenly he was there in front of my window, his head like a boulder, the huge bulk of his body moving up against the wall like a ship coming into port, searching . . . and then he stopped and I knew he'd seen me. He froze in place, magnificent, arrogant—he was so close I could hear him breathing—and then he started rubbing his chin and the side of his face against the wall. He wanted me to touch him. I'm as sure of this as I am of anything in my life: He wanted me to touch him. Ten seconds later he was gone, gliding out the screen door, up and over the fence—gone.

I spent today in the garage. I've never known it so hot. In the back corner I found some half-inch copper pipe. I cut seven pieces with the metal saw, each two feet long, then put them in the vise and filed the ends sharp as razors. I mixed some cement.

I can see where he takes the fence. Where the big paws come down. Where that great striped belly just strokes the dirt. I've planted them all in a row like a crop. A bed of pikes. Of copper teeth. The cement will take in three hours. I've gone out to check it twice. You make your place, draw your lines.

It's only three o'clock. I can hear the air conditioners roaring in the back rooms. You know it's bad when the glass on the windows feels hot to the touch. Some days I imagine it getting hotter and hotter till the sky turns red and the grass starts to smoke and the phone lines glow like hair in a fire.

Bramble Boy

Act One

I WANT TO BELIEVE THAT SOMETHING ENDURES. Because it has to. That something besides dreams survives the weight of our days.

This is how it was. On August 5, 1985, only a few hours after we'd picked a half bucket of blackberries in that tilting field where we used to find the pot plants hidden in the thorns— berries so crushable they seemed to disappear the more we picked—Laura and I dropped Carl off in Bakersfield, kissed him goodbye, and left for Delano. Fifteen minutes later we were dead. Detoured into woods we'd never seen before.

It shouldn't have happened. A moment's inattention, a quick swerve—the back of the semi coming at us like a rushing wall. In another world we would've driven back as the hot wind pushed in through the windows and found our boy asleep under his mobile of plastic butterflies.

Instead, at 9:30 that evening, the Bakersfield police received a phone call from someone named Rosa Gonzales at the Sunshine Day Care off Truxton. A fourteen-month-old baby named Carl Ruzika Jr. hadn't been picked up. No one answered at the parents' home number. The dispatcher on duty hunched over the metal desk and rubbed the bridge of his nose. He recognized the name.

"I'll have somebody there in ten," he said, already dreading the call to the grandparents in Porterville or the sister in Fresno, the confusion followed by the questions—desperate, clawing— and then the hysterics or anger or, worse, the weird politeness of people already crashing through to another life but still hearing themselves saying, "Yes, of course, no, I understand," and even, sometimes, "Thank you for calling."

He could've saved himself some pain—there'd be no phone call. There was nobody else, you see—no one at all: no parents, no surviving brothers or sisters, no friends beyond the daily round of work and beer and pay-per-view.

It's not something that occurs to people, this aloneness— everybody has somebody. When Rosa handed Carl in his miniature Padres cap to trooper Angela Lo that evening in Bakersfield, neither one imagined he was absolutely alone in the world, that like somebody looking down the line of selves in a department-store mirror, he could've looked down the generations stretching back through Denver and Gary to a little stucco house in Czechoslovakia, except that in his case, instead of dwindling with distance, the past would grow stronger, sprouting friends, relatives (even his own name regenerating roots—Carl to Karlík to Karlíček Ružička) while he stood at the vanishing point, orphaned by time.

And so, lost on the fruited plain, Carl became a ward of the State of California. He shat himself, he ate, he grew. As kids will. If the women who fed and changed and cared for him at the state-run children's home in Bakersfield tended to leave a little too often (overwhelmed or pregnant, following a boyfriend or running from one) having stayed just long enough for their going to hurt, they were, as a group, neither cold nor unkind. The Marys and Sallys and Amys and Toms did what they could, arranging the blocks, singing the songs, applying the antibiotic as needed. Birthdays came with cake and candles; the donated gifts were always wrapped. We were fine with them all.

Act Two

HE CAME TO LIVE WITH THE SEIKALYS, Ron and Ruth, in November of 1993, a quiet nine-year-old with a single suitcase and a blue, bulgy backpack with the head of a teddy bear sticking out of its zipper like it needed air. The Seikalys welcomed him to their home, Ron leading the way past the pickups and the goats and a long, sagging structure of warped boards and wire behind which a chicken drank from a white plastic bucket. Carl was the Seikalys' third, a year behind John and Anna. Ramon would come a year later, then Juanita and Cody. There were no set limits then on the number of foster kids a family could take in, and the Seikalys, with their big, wooden house on thirty-five acres, took their limit.

It didn't seem like an unhappy place. No different from all the other houses lost in the Sierra foothills, houses with driveways as rocky and pitted as old riverbeds, the Seikaly place, at first, seemed just fine. Busy as a summer camp even on those long

November Sundays when the fog dropped through the pines all day, it looked like the kind of place where everyone takes turns saying grace and washing the dishes, where everyone knows his role and pulls his weight—in short, a decent home. On winter weekdays, just after dawn, you'd always see three or four of the Seikaly kids waiting by the road in the rain, their raincoats hunched up from the packs underneath, two more crashing through the manzanita above the shallow, clattering river that used to be their drive.

It should've worked out. A new home, another life, the road unfolding like it should.

Whether Ron Seikaly was actually a cruel man or just a scared one doesn't really matter. Something about Carl just set him off—the way he'd never speak up so you could damn well hear him, the way he was always lookin' at you. The way he'd always hang back, livin' in his own head. While the other kids always snapped to—even Ramon, who could hardly speak a word of English—Carl couldn't seem to get away fast enough. The truth is, there was something about the boy—that weak voice, the thin wrists, the bad attitude—that made you want to wipe that judging look off his face.

Ron liked things to work the way he liked them to work— who didn't? He ran a tight ship—so what? It's not like he didn't explain his reasons. None of the others had a problem with it. Anyway, sparing the rod hadn't done much good since the days of the Bible.

People didn't really understand about Seikaly, men least of all. Seikaly was just the guy with the big forearms standing around telling bullshit stories about expertly decapitated rattlesnakes and Texas boar hunts so crammed with detail—"And there he is, squealin' like a stuck pig, my arrow stickin' outta his ass . . ."—that even those who knew better let it go. Though they didn't like him, though sometimes it felt like another, smaller man was hiding inside that big body, they gave him space, figuring that like a scared dog in a crowded room, he might bite for no reason at all.

Ruth was another story. A waitress at the Pine Grove Lodge, where she worked year-round, Ruth was a big woman with work-roughened elbows like peach pits and strong, doughy arms who didn't take shit from the tour operators or the murderous-looking cooks with their hair nets and their see-through gloves. In the winters the delivery guys would sit at her counter in their shirtsleeves, feeling good about themselves having just driven all the way up from the valley, and one and all, if you asked them, would tell you that Ruth—tough, shrewd Ruth—was a decent woman. A little hard, maybe, and not much on the jokes, but God-fearin' and decent.

WHO KNOWS WHAT went wrong, exactly? Or whether the trouble was the result of one accident or twenty? Maybe it had to do with the fact that Ron and Ruth were never Mommy and Daddy but always just Ron and Ruth, or that Carl, sitting on his bunk that first afternoon, started crying for no reason and kept on long after he should've stopped so that the rest of them, following Ron, went down to dinner without him. Maybe it was the way, from the very first, he was slow to answer Ron's questions, or the way he always lagged behind while the rest of them ran ahead. Maybe it was his stubbornness, or his laziness, or the way he'd bring home some dog-eared picture of a house or a pig and stand there, long after they'd said it was fine, wanting more, making himself pathetic. Maybe it was the way he looked at Ron the first time Ron smacked him across the face for having a smart mouth.

"Of all the kids, Carl was the only one gave us trouble," Ruth would say, wiping down the counter at the Pine Grove Lodge, bearing down, her left hand braced on the counter's edge. "We did everything we could, but after he got suspended for showin' off the knife Ron gave him for Christmas—after we'd *told* him about bringin' it to school—we'd had enough. Some kids, there's nothin' you can do—it's just one thing after another. So me and Ron, we made it very clear there's only so much we'd put up with, that he could either shape up or ship out, with our blessing."

Act Three

THE FIRST TIME CARL RAN AWAY HE WAS BACK before Ron even went to look for him, creeping past the chicken coop in the dark without the dogs barking and somehow sneaking into the house and up to his own bed as if hoping no one would notice he'd been gone. It was this last thing in particular, that he'd just crawl into his own bunk like nothing had happened, that set Ron off, and if he maybe came down a little heavier with the belt than usual, and kept goin' a little longer, his right arm rising and falling in short, quick strokes, raising welts like tic-tac-toe until the others, watching from the doorway, began to squirm and even Ruth started to say something, it's because when Ron'd swept his blankets aside he'd just laid there in his underwear, because he'd been expecting it, because he had no spunk, because he was ungrateful.

The second time he ran away he was gone almost four days. He was almost eleven by then. On the afternoon after they found he was gone, Ron called down to Fresno to report it, and the State Police came by and took a description and the next morning some Mexican woman from the agency came by and asked a lot of questions. Late that same night he was back, except this time Ron had had the kids lock all the doors and windows. He crept from one to the other like a thief, trying to find a way in, then curled up on the porch in his Padres jacket with the dirty collar and fell asleep.

Early the next morning Ron, alerted by Cody and Juanita, found him sleeping on a bed of newspapers that he'd pulled out of the garbage, his hands caught between his legs for warmth, and without a word grabbed him by the back of the neck, marched him across the yard and shoved him into the truck—or tried, because Carl grabbed the rim of the open door so that Ron had to tear him off and heave him in. According to Ruth, by the time they reached Fresno, the boy had worked himself into such a fit of remorse—babbling on about his room and his bear and how he'd be good now, please, just let him stay—that Ron, realizing it wouldn't look good to bring him in in that state, and worried about running into the same woman who'd come up the day before, relented and drove back.

And for a while, it almost looked like it might work out. Carl made his bed, he did his work, he said yes sir to Ron when Ron told him to do something, even smiled at the dinner table when one of the others said something funny. He tried to speak clearly, and to overcome his natural sullenness. And then one morning, while going through the kids' rooms, Ruth found a weird collection of fourteen glass jars filled with small, hard berries hidden in the back of his closet—some white, some brown, some as red as pomegranate seeds—and threw them out. That night, the rains came. The next morning he was gone.

IT WAS STILL dark when he came out on the two-lane below Badger holding the flashlight in the dripping sleeve of his jacket and sloshed through the cold brown water running down the road. He turned south toward the town of Lemon Cove, sixty miles away. The water in the ditch was moving fast with bits of bark and pine needles. He knew the rain would last for days, that having waited for so long, it would keep on till the hills swelled and burst and every gully showed to the bone. At first light he passed a hay barn and, cutting across the marshy field, crawled between two old bales that rose on either side of him like huge, protective beasts and fell asleep.

He spent the next day in the barn, huddled under a layer of straw. Around noon he took out the squares of cornbread he'd tucked under his T-shirt in a Ziploc bag to keep them dry. They'd gotten wet anyhow, so he ate half the yellow paste he found there, scooping it out with two fingers, then slipped the bag back in his shirt next to the smiling bear and fell asleep again. When he woke up it was dark, and he got up and pulled on his hood and walked out into the rain. He turned right at the road, stepping carefully around the slippery washouts where the mud fanned out, ducking off the road whenever headlights came over the rise or around the curves, too cold to think that somebody checking on their stock might see a small light walking in all that darkness and know or guess who it was and put in a call to Ron.

WHEN HE HUNG UP the phone she tried to stop him, shouting, "Ron, call the agency, Ron, he's not worth it, Ron, let him go," shouting from the porch as the truck's headlights opened up the dark, the rain coming down thick and straight, shouting till the tires bit the muddy gravel and he was gone. She watched the lights turn at the road like a beast turning its head, and started to shiver.

Whether it was because of the rain or the turn in the road or both, he didn't hear the pickup until it was behind him, its lights turned off, the sound of its motor familiar and terrifying and he was running into the dark hearing his name yelled like he'd never heard anybody's name yelled before, hearing the truck door slam and the quick sound of boots on gravel, running until a branch took him hard across the neck and his flashlight went flying and a heavy hand grabbed his shoulder and lifted him straight off the ground. Something hit him across the face, then hit him again, then a third time, and kicking out into the exploding dark he was suddenly down and plunging blindly over the dirt.

And then he felt them, and dropping to all fours he plowed straight into that field of brambles, burrowing in, feeling the vines closing up tight behind him, their thorny arms as strong as wire. Behind him he could hear Seikaly, snared in inch-thick ropes cutting into his scalp, his throat, his face, stumbling and cursing like a man fighting somebody he couldn't see. When Carl couldn't go any farther he curled into a ball and lay very still. After a while the cursing turned to whimpering, then pleading, then stopped.

A warm breath of air brought the smell of earth and mildewed wood, touched his face and was gone.

The Angels Come
to Panorama Heights

I NEVER BOUGHT THE HARD-MAN ACT—the pissed-off voice, the gunslinger walk, the harelip that stuck out his jaw like he was giving you one free shot before he broke your face, "C'mon, right here" . . . I just figured he'd been doing it so long he believed it himself. I had a PhD in frauds, all that dick-swinging bullshit, the arm around the shoulders: You're gonna teach me how to be a man? I don't think so.

In '69 I was twenty-two, a year older than Jackson Browne, and the Central Valley was still all John Birch and Jesus and the Skoal seal of approval stamped on your ass, but at least it wasn't Scranton. I had a job babysitting seventeen-year-olds who hadn't made the right life choices, and after a week of character building with a mattock and a twelve-pound sledge I'd drive them up to Panorama Heights, where Don Kinch, the owner, put a hole in one of them with a cigarette just two weeks before fate decided to pay him a visit. Kinch, I mean.

But Wayne Senior, formerly of Scranton, PA, now retired to Florence (supermax federal pen) would say you need to set up a story like you would a joke, and I'll give him that—he knew about jokes—so let me get this right. Do the old man proud.

FIRST OFF, THERE was no panorama—you can call anything anything—just an old, converted house with a double-deep porch five thousand feet up in the Sierra foothills and two hours out of Bakersfield. Except for the bar, there wasn't much: a cold, little pool with bugs, a couple of outbuildings, a horse mowing the weeds. You'd step out of your truck, your shirt sticking to your back, and the first thing you'd hear over the knocking of the engine would be the dogs on the porch staking their claim—the second thing would be the quiet. The sun smelled like sage and pine. A cool breeze moved the shade over the busted recliners on the porch. Twenty yards past the dirt parking lot was a turnaround. From here, going on meant going back.

The bar wasn't that different from any other in the Sierra: walking in you'd see a half dozen white shirts sitting in the dark, sleeves bent forward at the elbows, then the old guys inside them, bootheels hooked on their stools. After that maybe the diamond-back skin pegged to the wall above the cooler, the eight-point mulie looking stupid in a sombrero—the usual crap. There was a pool table, a jukebox. A map of all the whorehouses in Nevada. Tacked to the ceiling was a poster of Wile E. Coyote with his hand around roadrunner's neck and his dick up his butt. BEEP, BEEP, MY ASS, it said.

I liked the bar, the chill, sharp smell of wood and beer. I liked the porch. I came up by myself the first time—my day off. When I walked in, everybody got quiet. I nodded, took a seat at the bar, the sweat cooling on my back. I felt like I'd walked into a redneck skit. A handwritten sign above the bottles said, IF YOU HAVE SOMETHING TO SELL, LEAVE. Another, scotch-taped to the cash register read, DON'T EVEN ASK.

The old guys to my left had gone back to the pros and cons of driving down to the valley when a small, sharp woman wearing a pair of man-sized glasses came in from the kitchen and started rearranging the bottles. I was looking at a man's dress shoe hanging from a nail by a wire when somebody started yelling somewhere out back. Roaring might be a better word.

Nobody seemed to notice.

"Somethin' to eat?" the woman said to the mirror.

The voice was closer now, throttle open, fuck-me-blind furious.

I asked what I could have.

"I can warm up a chili side if you want it."

"Gotta figure in your gas," the guy to my left said.

A door slammed, then slammed again, making the bottles tink like this brass contraption my mother used to set up on Christmas which used the heat of the candles to turn five angels hung from little hooks. I used to watch them go in circles. Each angel had a thin gold wand dangling from a hole in its leg that tapped against a tiny triangle as it came around—tink, tink, tink.

"Five bucks a tank, that's a bag of feed right there," the other guy said.

It hit like that crack of thunder that makes you jump sitting at the dinner table: "*Goddammit, getyerheadouttayrerassthen!*"

"You'd have to take that in account," the first guy said, like he was deaf.

"*Here, gimmethat, dumbass.*" A loud bang came from some- where in the kitchen, followed by a solid crash and a satisfied grunt. "*There. How's that?*"

The woman with the glasses came in and set down my food. "Hot sauce?"

"*You call that a wrench?*" There was another bang, another crash, followed by the sound of something metal ricocheting around a small room. "*Jaheezus Christ!*"

Presently a man—graying, fiftyish, solid six feet—strode in from the kitchen and turning his back on the room, began to shuffle the bottles the woman had just finished rearranging.

"Don," mumbled the men at the bar, almost at the same time. There was no response.

"Breakin' in the new kid, huh?" said the man to my left, and two or three others down the line chuckled carefully.

No answer.

I smiled to myself: no better way to fuck with you than don't answer: Soon it's Daddy, what did I do? Daddy, what's the mat- ter? A little more of that and it's Daddy, please, Daddy, say something, Daddy, I'm sorry.

"You want another?" He was standing in front of me, jaw out, hands on the bar like he was holding it down. His voice, rough as a rasp, seemed to explode past the harelip and up through his nose.

I tilted the glass, thought about it. "Sure."

He took the beer, turned to the tap. He had it down: No give, no take. Zero interest in you. No wasted motion. He scooped a handful of peanuts and threw them in his mouth. With the thick chest hair, the flannel half out of his jeans like he'd just won a wrestling match, he seemed like something made to go off, hoping for a match.

"Heard you have a swimming pool up here, man," I said, because I'd be the match.

He snorted. "Who told you that?"

"Some guy in Glenville."

He wiped down the counter, threw the rag into a bucket. "And you believed him?"

The room—his audience—was following along.

"No reason not to."

He put the beer down in front of me. "To believe that you'd have to be from Glenville." He leaned forward, still chewing, indicated the room with a jerk of his head. "Let me ask you somethin'," he said, the words coming out in little explosions: "This PLACE look like it'd have a POOL to you?"

I looked around, let him wait. "Not really," I said.

"Well, there you have it," he said, and walked down the bar.

The woman with the glasses came back in and took my plate. "Be somethin' else?"

I shook my head.

"Buck even."

"How come?"

"Seventy-five for your food, quarter for the pool."

I nodded slowly.

She rang the register open. "Don't have a suit, there's some cutoffs somebody left might fit you—you look skinny enough."

Kinch was drawing another beer. "And shut the gate or the horses will shit on the grass," he said, not looking up.

IT WAS A good joke—I didn't mind. I started bringin' my crew on Saturdays, climbing up from the valley to that huge shaded porch, that ratty little pool. It was a mutually beneficial arrangement: The pool was good for my guys, and when I tired of listenin' to kids going on about shit they knew nothing about I'd take a beer to the porch and read a book—I had a year of junior college under my belt. As for Kinch, we were big business. He recognized me now, exchanged a few words.

"College, huh?" he said, after he asked and I told him.

I wanted him to say something ignorant about intellectuals having their heads up their asses. "That's right," I said. "I'm gonna finish my degree when I get back east."

He scribbled something on a pad, put the pencil behind his ear, punched open the register. "Good for you," he said.

THE THING WITH the cigarette didn't happen till the third week. By then I'd heard all the stories from the locals who drove all the way from Oildale just to be crapped on by the big man: How Kinch had done this, how Kinch had done that, how he'd hit a guy so hard once he looked like a movie running backward before he crashed through the window and onto the porch.

"That so?" I'd say.

The guy would take a pull of his beer, set it down, put number ten in the corner pocket. "Not somebody you want to piss off."

Nods and grunts all around.

"I'll remember that."

"See that shoe?"

"So?"

"Don took that shoe off a guy doin' life in Folsom."

"How'd he get in there?"

"What? No—before. He took it off him before."

"Got it."

It was funny, really—the same thing everywhere you went: Men trying on poses, voices, the local badass noticing his forearm in the glass, flexing the wrist just a little . . . there, perfect!—everybody playing bigger than they felt while trying to figure out what "bigger" meant. Sometimes it was just easier to get together and get bigger by proxy—nominate a hero. Enter: Kinch. Kinch was their Gary Cooper, walking to meet the train, their harelipped David, swingin' that sling. They loved him, groveled at his feet to make it real. He made it possible for them to back down and pucker up—*You want this job?*—because *he'd* never back down, never calculate the odds, because he'd piss on the devil if the devil came callin'—and put his red ass out too.

I didn't argue. I didn't tell 'em that in real life Gary Cooper takes a bullet in the throat, that Goliath steps on David's head on the way to dinner. If anything I felt sorry for Kinch, forced to play that part year in and year out. Legend? Lord and master? I'd seen the real man that morning with the cigarette—he was the same as everybody else. Which was about as surprising as learning Killer Kowalski faked his shit in the WWWF, or Superman held down a second job selling tires in Wilkes-Barre.

What happened with the cigarette was every Saturday my crew would line up in front of the cash register and Camilla, Don's wife, would take the money and stamp their wrists to show they'd paid for the pool. That morning she was out, so Don took over, cigarette in his teeth, mashing the stamp into the pad like he wanted to punch through the counter. I was coming up the steps when I heard one of my kids scream, and Kinch bellowing, "Why didn't you move? What the fuck is *wrong* with you?"

It didn't take long to figure out what happened: Kinch, switching out his cigarette for the stamp as a joke, had expected this kid, Ralph, to pull his hand away, but Ralph was a special boy. Ralph just looked at him. Kinch had moved the cigarette closer, slow-motion. Ralph smiled that "go ahead and burn me" smile. So Kinch, being Kinch, put a black-rimmed hole in his wrist.

I got pretty worked up about it, threatened to take my kids and never come back. This was a government program, for Christ's sake; I couldn't have kids showing up with cigarette burns. And I saw it in his eyes: confusion, uncertainty. "What the fuck is wrong with him?" he kept yelling. "All he had to do is move."

It just so happened there was plenty wrong with Ralph, a hundred-eighty-pounder with soft Michelin Man wrists who entertained himself by inventing tortures for everybody he knew—"I know what I'd do to you, Wayne," he'd say to me on the way to the mess hall—but that was not the point. The point was that Ralph had called Kinch's bluff, and Kinch'd been rattled by it. *That* was the point.

He came up to talk to me that afternoon as I ate at the bar by myself.

"Want another?" he said, wiping down the counter.

I shook my head.

"How's that kid's hand?"

"He'll live."

He nodded, breathing through his nose like a bull. "Listen, I—"

"Don't worry about it," I said.

He stood there, trying to figure out his next move—nobody's terror.

I don't know why I decided to let him off the hook. "He's a weird little punk," I said.

He grunted, moved on down the bar.

"Let me know if you want another," he said.

It was the tone. For a split second it was just the two of us, just me and him. It made me uncomfortable. It was like at the zoo when the orangutan stops picking its nose and suddenly you're looking into these human eyes, trapped inside that hide, and you get this jolt of recognition and disgust.

HOWEVER IT WAS, you could almost admire the way Kinch held up his end, grunting and bellowing and bullying like a champ, riding herd on those poor bastards who paid good money just to bask in his ridicule. And the truth is he might have gone on doing just that except for the law that says there's *always* a bigger fish. Always. A sudden lunge, a quick flare of gills, and all that's left of yesterday's big boy is a thoughtful

look in the eyes of the victor and a single silver scale drifting
to the sand.

FOR DON KINCH of Panorama Heights the law kicked in fast
on July 26, 1969. The temperature in Porterville hit 116. I'd have
liked to have been there. I was at Panorama Heights instead.

You could hear them five miles out, people said, like something out of the Bible—seventy, eighty machines roaring down
5 out of Stockton where they'd left one man dead and another
unlikely to do much of anything ever again. Traffic on the inter-
state, seeing them come up in the rearview, filling it, pulled over
on the shoulder and let them pass.

There was never going to be an easy answer to this one. A
quarter mile long, they roared through Visalia, then Delano.
The local cops, each with their one or two cruisers, wisely hung
back. By one o'clock, thirty-five squad cars from four jurisdic-
tions formed a roadblock at the merge of 99 and 65. By one thirty
they'd realized their mistake. The Angels, like a headless snake,
had veered into the foothills.

I don't know why nobody picked up the phone that afternoon. I can see the people on the other end clamping the receiv-
ers with their shoulders, groping for the shotgun shells—not
able to hear if the phone's ringing or anybody's picked up, yelling get out just get the hell out. Camilla may have been in the
kitchen. My guys were by the pool making idiots of themselves
in front of two high-school girls up from Poso Creek.

It happened very quickly.

"The hell is that noise?" said somebody at the bar.

"Not a saw."

"What's the matter with the dogs?" said somebody else.

And then they were there, pouring over the rise, thunder filling the bar like water in an aquarium, and we just sat there looking at each other, trying to understand what was happening and then I was running for the back even as my guys were crowding in from the pool and I was yelling, "Go, go, get the fuck out of here—just go," but by then they were everywhere.

There was nothing to do. This wasn't some Marlon Brando bullshit. They filled the bar with their leather and skulls, red-eyed, strung-out, too many, too fucked up to care about anything at all, shoving toward the back while we sat there trying not to breathe, to be. I heard a dog yelp outside.

"Where's Don?" I heard somebody whisper, and my heart, like a spasming muscle, jumped at the thought and was still. All fairy tales ended. This one ended here, with eighty Angels doing whatever the fuck they wanted to whoever they wanted because they could. The only thing that could make it worse was for Kinch to come in, playing his role. I found myself praying he'd stay away. I didn't want to have to watch him go down, flailing, holding on to his myth like it could protect him, like it meant something.

The crowd heaved and swayed, packed to the walls, yelling for beer. Toward the back a commotion kicked up and I saw a biker's arms come up twice like a conductor's as he stomped something on the floor.

He strode in from the kitchen wiping his hands on a rag, the usual look of disgust on his face. Turning his back on the crowd, he rearranged some bottles, scooped a handful of peanuts, threw them in his mouth, then took the convict's shoe off the nail and smashed it on the wood till the room got quiet. "I'll say it once," he announced, big hands out like he was holding down the bar: "Two BITS a glass, no BEER or BAREASS by the POOL, no—" He stopped chewing. A biker, his massive arms bulging out of his sleeveless leather jacket, had hoisted himself up on the pool table.

"Hey, you," Kinch roared, the words shooting out of his nose like bullets. "Ass off the TABLE or get the FUCK outta my place!"

TWENTY YEARS LATER, when I returned to Panorama Heights, it was a bed and breakfast. The porch was gone, the parking lot paved. The brown mat in front of the door said GOD BLESS OUR HOME. I didn't go in.

"Don Kinch? Sure, died of a heart attack in '86," said the man who answered the door. "Camilla moved to Arizona."

I thanked him, went back to my car. I looked at the oaks, feeling the back of my shirt unstick from my back, then started the long drive back to the valley.

It didn't matter. There'd be some of us who'd remember, who'd forever see him walking into that bar exactly, and I mean *exactly* the way he'd walked into it a thousand times before, who still wondered what he could have been thinking at that moment when in fact he probably wasn't thinking anything at all.

"HEY, YOU," Kinch roared, the words shooting out of his nose like bullets. "Ass off the TABLE or get the FUCK outta my place!"

After a moment's pause, the biker jumped down off the pool table. Kinch, satisfied, turned to the tap and began drawing beers, then turned again just in time to see the man take out his dick and begin pissing on the floor.

There was no pause, no break. Putting down the beer, Kinch came out from behind the bar, the crowd parting like iron shavings from the wrong end of a magnet, walked right up and hit the guy (who was either too stunned or stoned to move) with a straight-from-the-shoulder right to the face so thunderous, so uninhibited, it sent the man staggering across the floor like a home movie run backward, flipped him over a table and laid him out cold.

Kinch returned to the bar, reached under it, placed the 12-gauge on the wood. I ain't gonna say it again," he said. "Two BITS a beer, no BOOZE or BAREASS by the pool, no tab at the BAR." He tossed a rag in the general direction of the pool table. "And clean up that mess," he roared.

And they did.

Bakersfield

IF YOU WERE A FIFTEENTH-CENTURY SAINT out walking the billowing fields of heaven on July 24, 1985, and you happened to look down out of the sky over the Owens Valley, you'd have seen a twenty-two-year-old ranch hand named Jack Henderson sleeping against the cinder-block wall of the Lone Pine Laundry. A tough kid with a big, calloused heart, he'd picked this place because it was hidden behind a kind of brick corral containing five metal garbage cans and because, three days earlier, he'd met and fallen in love with a dark-haired girl named Janie Sanders, whose window looked out over the place he slept. That morning the two of them were running away to Bakersfield, starting early to beat the heat.

Sleeping on his side, both arms caught between his legs, Jack rolled to his back and opened his eyes to a sky still dark but bluing fast. Two small clouds, like commas, hurried across that open space. To the west, the Sierra was dark as a woodcut.

Stretching his legs against the warm bottom of the sleeping

bag, he put his hands behind his head, breathing in the chill smell of sage. Somebody was making coffee. When he turned his head, his jacket smelled like her hair and old smoke and he gathered it up to his face and breathed deep. In an hour the sun coming over the Inyo Range would break on the peaks, then seep into the broken bowl of the valley.

By then they'd be on their way. They'd talked about it, planned it, giddy with the thought of it. Janie and Jack. Home hadn't been home for either of them for years, his like a ship that's made up its mind to drink itself to death, hers nothing but sadness and screaming. They'd thought they'd never get away.

Bakersfield was the answer. There were jobs there. They could see it. They'd get a small house, and a dog, and on hot summer nights after work they'd drive down to the Kern with a bottle and a blanket and wade up the shoals in the moonlight.

Sometimes he'd felt like there was something in the world that didn't want you to be free, a headwind that picked up as soon as you started to run, but two nights ago, sitting on the roof of the wooden dugout passing a bottle of wine and watching twelve-year-olds fumble grounders in the glare of the stadium lights, he'd felt something happening to him— something good and true and right. Before the game was over the two of them had climbed down the chain-link fence, then cut between the motel and the Rock Shop into the great open room of the desert.

They'd walked toward the moon coming up over the Inyos, their arms around each other's waists, following the coyote trails that wound between the rabbit brush, and after they'd taken what they needed from each other on the blanket they'd spread on the flat lake bed, as they lay tangled up, her breasts flat against his chest and her leg slipped between his like they'd been sleeping together for years, everything felt changed. For both of them. The moon had lit the Sierra, and sitting up in the middle of that huge space they saw how small the town's lights looked beneath the mountains and the sky.

The light was coming on, and with things quickly taking shape around him he slipped on his boots, standing on the bag to keep the burrs out of his socks, then pulled on the flannel he'd left folded on his duffel and carefully rolled his bag. At a faucet sticking out of the back wall of the laundry he splashed water on his face and hair, then rolled down his sleeves and put on his jacket. The day ahead wasn't going to be a lot of fun—he knew that. By seven the coolness would be gone. By eight the air would smell like tar and roadkill. By ten everything along the road—the telephone poles, the wires, the three miles of black rock escarpment stretching along 395—would be wavering and doubling in the heat like something inside was struggling to get loose.

The first step was to make the turnoff—maybe fifty miles. Next came the two-lane running up through the boulder fields to the town of Lake Isabella—another twenty. Last was what the locals called Canyon Boulevard, a no-name dirt road hacked into the cliff so narrow that people who drove it would stop and honk before taking a turn. He'd never liked it—the drop, the river roaring over the boulders a hundred feet below, the way it drew your eye. Still, it'd save them four, maybe five hours. If they got a ride, they'd be home free.

He looked up. The light was on in the window above the laundry.

Carrying the suitcase down the wooden steps she glanced up quickly to smile and wave, then steadied herself on the wooden railing. She hadn't slept, really—it didn't matter. They were going. She felt excited yet strangely calm. She loved this man and he loved her—nothing else mattered. Let them come after her: By the time they found the note she'd be gone.

Waiting in the alley, he watched her disappear through the back door of the diner, then reappear with a paper bag and a cup of coffee. A woman he didn't know, her sleeves rolled up her big arms, came out the screen door and watched them walk away. When Janie waved from the end of the alley, the woman raised her right hand just past her waist, then brought it slowly down.

THEY HADN'T BEEN waiting more than a minute when a battered pick-up, its lights still on, pulled over on the gravel. As they walked up, an older man in work-broken jeans and a clean white shirt leaned over to roll down the passenger-side window.

"I got her wired so she don't open," he said, "but you're welcome to get in back if you like."

They thanked him and climbed up into the bed with spools of bailing wire, a posthole digger, and three bags of cement.

"Just move that stuff over," he called out the window, then waited for them to make a space and settle in. The fence posts accelerated. They were gone.

"How you feelin'?" he yelled over the wind, smiling.

She put the coffee down and kissed him long and hard, her hair whipping around them both. It was falling back—the rage, the sadness, the TV voices laughing in the desert heat. They'd never find them now. Through the back window of the truck Jack could see the man reach for the glove compartment, pull out a pack of cigarettes, tap one out against the wheel, then dip his head.

Two miles over their heads a ripped postage stamp of snow showed white against the rock.

They'd been standing on the road less than twenty minutes when the second ride—another pickup—pulled up a quarter mile ahead and began backing up the shoulder. They yelled "gracias," then climbed in with three kids sitting on sacks of feed, and Janie talked to the oldest, a girl maybe ten years old holding a round-faced baby.

"I didn't know you could talk Spanish," he shouted over the wind as she offered the kids the biscuits from the diner.

He watched the baby crumble the biscuit in its soaking fist. The sun rose over the Inyos, covering the valley in low, red light.

It could be done—he'd always known that. If you had the heart and the balls you could walk out, just slip your life like the gopher snake he'd once watched rub itself open on a piece of rock in an old fish-tank; the eyes had peeled back, the pattern on the new skin separated off from the one above it, and the snake had crawled out of its own jaws, fresh as the day.

TURNING AWAY FROM the dust, they listened to the truck with the kids pull away, then picked their bags off the gravel.

"We're makin' good time," he said.

"I still can't believe we're doin' this."

A truck pushing a wall of hot air went by, then a van packed with men who looked at them as they passed. A half mile down, the van's brake lights flashed on, then off. After that, nothing. The sun was up now, the air on the horizon turning white. Five miles east, out past the sage and the tumbleweed scraping against itself in the sluggish wind, the alkali flats were pink as plastic.

"Feel like walkin'?" he said. "How's that suitcase?"

Holding hands, they started walking, the duffel over his shoulder, the suitcase bumping her leg, stopping every hundred steps to let her switch hands or to drink from one of the soda bottles.

"You all right?" he asked. "You want me to take that?"

"I'm fine," she said, flushed, smiling at him. He leaned under the straw hat and kissed her, then wiped his forehead with his sleeve.

THEY WATCHED IT coming across the flats, a big white car dragging a wall of dust.

"Wonder where *he's* goin'?" she said as the car braked hard on the gravel, then fishtailed out on the highway and roared by.

"Wherever it is," he said, taking a bottle out of the duffel, "you can bet your ass he's not . . ."

But the car had stopped, was even now waiting for them, its brake lights showing red through the settling dust.

"Well, I'll be goddamned," he said.

It was a big car, an old Chevy Impala. As they ran up the shoulder the motor turned off and a thick-necked, sandy-haired man wearing brown office pants and a short-sleeved shirt stepped heavily out into the highway.

"Thanks," said Jack. "Gettin' hot out here."

"Why don't you kids put your stuff in here?" the man said, opening the trunk. "That way you can sit together in back."

He couldn't say why he hesitated. He could feel her looking at him as he dropped the duffel in the trunk and piled her suitcase on top of it.

"Mind if we bring the water?" he called out to the man, who was already climbing into the car.

"Bring whatever you like."

She looked at him before they climbed in, reading his face, silently mouthing the question. He shrugged. "I think so," he said, then got in before her, sliding over on the seat.

As though suddenly aware of his responsibility, the man accelerated gently to sixty, then eased off on the gas.

"Comfortable back there?" he said.

"Fine. Thanks for the ride."

"I'll be honest with you, I'm glad for the company."

"Works for us."

"Hard day."

"Sorry to hear it."

He watched the man's face in the rearview: maybe fifty, soft, like a weightlifter going to fat. Hair the color of dust. A heavy arm lay over the back of the passenger seat like there was somebody sitting there.

"Where you kids from?"

"Tahoe. You?"

"Little place about an hour back. You wouldn't know it."

They rode in silence. Jack watched the man take a long breath, saw his eyes, staring at a spot on the dashboard, lose their focus, then wrench themselves back into the present.

"So where you headed, anyway?" he said.

"Bakersfield," Janie said.

"That so? What's in Bakersfield?"

"Don't know. We're hopin' jobs, maybe a place of our own—"

"Pretty much everything," Jack said.

A yellow jacket blown in through the window was beating itself against the glass, and taking the hat off Janie's head, Jack shooed it out into the hot wind, then handed back the hat and leaning in gave her a quick kiss.

"That's nice," the man said.

"What's that?" Jack said.

"—two of you like that, everything figured out."

"You know how it is," Jack said.

"What would make you say that?"

Though Jack's thumb never stopped drawing little circles around the knuckle of her hand, something inside him suddenly crouched down.

"I think all he meant was—" Janie started to say.

"Hey, I didn't mean to make you uncomfortable," the man said. Switching hands on the wheel, he took the unmarked turn-off for Lake Isabella. "I just meant, you know, not everybody's so lucky. Some people's horse never leaves the gate."

The weight of his arm on the seat had tattooed a grid into the soft skin.

Feeling Janie squeeze his hand, Jack turned slowly, aware that the man could see him in the rearview, and nodded, looking past her so it would look like he was just nodding to some music in his head. Everything was fine. The double-wides were show-ing up along the road now. They passed a man bent under the hood of a truck, two little kids riding bicycles on a dirt driveway.

"So . . . Bakersfield," the man said suddenly, like he'd been thinking about it the whole time.

"That's the plan anyway," Jack said.

"It's good to have a plan."

"I think so."

"And you've got each other—that's the most important thing."

"Guess it is."

"Count on it."

They stopped at an intersection. A woman in a blue pickup pulled out of a gas station.

The man tapped his fingers on the steering wheel.

"You hear about that woman in Tulare accidentally drove over her own kid?" he said.

"Oh my God, that was terrible," Janie said. "Said she looked away for, like, a second—that she was just backing up so she could put the lawnmower in the garage."

"Guess she'll need a new plan," the man said.

The light changed.

NONE OF THEM said anything as they drove out of Lake Isa-bella, then turned off on an unmarked dirt road that ran along a barbed-wire fence spotted with trash. The tires clanged over a cattle guard. A hundred feet ahead, the earth dropped away.

Two dented signs leaning in the loose soil read, DANGER—NOT A MAINTAINED ROAD, and 10 MPH. A third, handwritten on a piece of board nailed to a fence post said: I LOVE YOU, JOHN.

The man took off his sunglasses. "This next bit is a little tricky," he said.

Far above the canyon's rim, a hawk circled the sun, hunting the shadows below.

They drove out onto a road like the ledge on a skyscraper— no fence, no shoulder, nothing but air to the right—then edged around a corner so tight that from fifty feet away it looked like the road simply disappeared into the wall.

"Oh my God," she said, gripping his hand.

"Yeah," Jack said.

"How long does this go for?"

"Not that long. Don't look."

"Oh Jesus," she said. Two feet of dirt separated the tires and the canyon air.

"I don't like it either," Jack said. "Don't look."

"Sometimes things don't work out," the man said suddenly.

"I'm wonderin' if I could ask you to slow down a little," Jack said.

"Like when you're young you think you can snap your fingers and the world'll come runnin' like a dog—"

"I'm wonderin' if you wouldn't mind slowin' down a little."

"—an' then you realize *you're* the dog, and everything you thought is different."

"Sir, could you—?"

"Like all you're here for is to get beat on."

"Oh, my God," Jack heard her whimper. "Oh, Jesus."

"Please, I don't know what you're doin' but— "

The car scraped sickeningly against the rock wall of the cliff, lurched right. A little strip of white, far below, came out of the canyon wall, then went back.

He turned to look at them, his face unreadable as Christ's, his voice resigned yet curious: "I gotta be honest with you—I don't know about this next one." He smiled. "But hey, maybe you're lucky."

He stomped on the brakes. As the car began to slide sideways toward the green light of the canyon, Janie started to scream.

WHEN THE ROAD opened into the sun the man pulled over on the shoulder, took their things out of the trunk and drove away. Jack could barely stand. Janie clung to him, crying into his chest, her sobs somehow self-conscious in the silence.

Unable to speak, soaked in sweat, Jack looked down the empty highway, then up into the sky. High above their heads, the hawk scored a circle around the sun. For just a second, as if remembering some foolish, drunken thought, he saw them, their pants rolled up to their knees, wading up the shoals in the moonlight.

Crossing

IT WAS RAINING WHEN THEY DROVE OUT OF TACOMA that morning. When the first car appeared he could see it from a long way off, dragging a cloud of mist like a parachute, and when it passed them he touched the wipers to clear things up and his mind flashed to a scene of a black road, still wet, running toward mountains larded with snow like fatty meat. For some reason it made him happy, and he hadn't been happy in a while. By seven the rain was over. The line of open sky in the east was razor sharp.

He looked over at the miniature jeans, the sweatshirt bunched beneath the seat belt's strap, the hiking boots dangling off the floor like weights. "You OK?" he said. "You have to pee?" He slowed and drove the car onto the shoulder and the boy got out to pee. He looked at him standing on that rise in the brome and the bunchgrass, his little hips pushed forward. When the boy walked back to the car he swung the door open for him, then reached over and pulled the door shut and bumped out on the empty road.

Not much had changed, really. A half an hour out of

Hoquiam he began to see the clear-cuts through the firs, a strange, white light, as if the world dropped away fifty feet out from the pavement. The two of them had been talking about what to do if you saw a mountain lion (don't run, never run), and what they'd have for lunch. He hoped the boy wouldn't notice. Twenty minutes later they were past it, and the light behind the trees had disappeared.

He'd been at the house just after dawn, like he'd promised. He sat in the driveway for a while looking at the yard, the azaleas he'd planted, the grass in the yard beaten flat by the rain. For a long time he hadn't wanted her back, hadn't wanted much of anything, really. He went inside, wiping his shoes and ducking his head like a visitor and when the boy came running into the living room he threw him over his shoulder, careful not to hit his head on the corner of the TV, and at some point he saw her watching them, leaning against the kitchen counter in her bathrobe, and when he looked at her she shook her head and looked away and at that moment he thought, maybe. Maybe he could make this right. One step at a time.

THE FOREST SERVICE road had grown over so much that only his memory of where it had been told him where to turn. The last nine miles would take them an hour. This is it, kid, his old man would say whenever they turned in. You excited? Every year. The car lurched and swayed, the grass hissing against the undercarriage. It'd thrown him when the old man had died, though he couldn't say why, really. Tough bastard, he could give him that. He could see him, standing in the river hacking his lungs out, laying out an eighty-foot line. "Almost there," he said to the little boy next to him. "You excited?"

He slowed under the trees to let his eyes adjust and when he rolled down the window the air shoved in and he could hear the white noise of the river. God how he needed this place, the nests of vines like something scratched out, the furred trunks, soft with rot. He'd been waiting for this a long time. A low vine scraped against the roof. He smiled. Go ahead and scrape, you fucker, he thought, scrape it all.

EIGHT YEARS. It didn't seem that long. Where the valley widened out he could see what the winter had left behind: the gouged-out pools, the sixty-foot trunks rammed into the deadfalls, the circles of upturned roots like giant blossoms of Queen Anne's lace . . . A gust of warmer air shoved in: vegetation, sunlight, the slow fire of decay. Sometimes it wasn't so easy to know how to go, how to keep things alive. Sometimes the vise got so tight you could forget there was anything good left in the world. But this was good. He'd been talking about this place—the rivers, the elk, the steelhead in the pools—since the boy was old enough to understand. And now here it was. He looked at the water, rushing slowly like flowing glass over car-sized boulders nudged together like eggs.

He explained it all as they lay out their things in the mossy parking place at the road's end. The trail continued across the Quinault; they'd ford the river, then walk about three miles to an old settler's barn where they could spend the night. They'd set up their tent anyway because the roof was pretty well gone.

Of course they'd have a campfire—there was a fire ring right there—and sometimes, if you were quiet, herds of elk would come into the meadow at dusk.

When they came out of the trees and onto the stony beach he felt a small shock, as if he were looking at a house he'd grown up in but now barely recognized. The river was bigger than he remembered it, stronger; it moved like a swiftly flowing field. He didn't remember the opposite shore being so far off. He stood there, listening to it seething in its bed, to the inane chatter of the pebbles in the shallows, the hollow tock of the stones knocking against one another in the deeper water. Downstream, a branch caught in a deadfall reared up like something shot, then tore loose. For a moment he considered pulling out, explaining . . . but there was nowhere else to go. And he'd promised.

"Well, there she is," he said.

They took off their packs and squatted down next to each other on the embankment. "You want to take your time, kiddo," he said. "People in a hurry get in trouble." The boy nodded, very serious. He'd bring their packs over and then come right back for him. It would take a little while, but he'd be able to see him the whole time. He'd wave when he got to the other side.

He took off his pants and socks and boots, stuffed the pants and socks into the top of the pack, then tied the boots back on over his bare feet. The boy's weightless blue backpack, fat with his sleeping bag and teddy bear, he strapped to the top as well, then swung the whole thing on his back. No belt. He looked at the boy. "First rule of river crossing—never buckle your waist belt. If you go down, you have to be able to get your pack off as quickly as possible, OK?" The boy nodded. "I'll be right back," he said.

It wasn't too bad. He took it slow, carefully planting the stick downstream with his right arm, resisting the urge to look back. Ten yards out the water rose above his knees and he slowed even more, feeling for the edges of the rocks with his boots, moving from security to security. The heavier current swept the stick before it touched the bottom, making it harder to control, and he began drawing it out and stabbing it down ahead of himself and slightly upstream to make up for the drift, and then he was on the long, gravelly flat and across. He threw down the packs and looked back. The boy was just where he'd left him, sitting on the rocks, hugging his knees. He waved quickly and started back. You just had to be careful. So what do you do if you fall? he remembered asking once—how old could he have been, seventeen?—and the old man calling back over his shoulder, "Don't fuckin' fall."

The second crossing, with the boy on his back, was actually easier. They talked the whole time, and he made his way carefully, steadily, feeling the skinny legs bouncing against his thighs, leaning into the hands buckled across his collarbone, and halfway across, with the hot smell of the pines coming from the shore and the sun strong on his face, he knew he'd made it out the other side. Where had it come from—this slide into weakness, this vision of death like a tunnel at the end of the road and no way to get off or turn around? It didn't matter. Whatever it was had passed. He'd rebuild it all—one step at a time. He and his son would be friends. Nothing mattered more.

THE BARN WAS just where he remembered it, standing against the trees like a rib cage. What could they have been thinking, building a barn in a jungle with ninety inches of rain a year? Its roof was half gone and its floor rotted through but there was something about pitching a tent inside that skeleton that was pretty neat, they agreed, and snapping the compression poles together—always a good trick—he remembered the two of them working together, quietly, easily, then his father crawling into the tent to lay out the sleeping bags. Something about rooms in rooms.

They set up the rain fly just in case, then shined the flashlight at the bats clustered under the peak of the roof, making them squeak like kittens, and went outside to the fire ring. It was a beautiful evening, still and perfect, the sky above the grass deepening to the blue of a butterfly wing he'd once found by the side of a trail in Guatemala, and they took turns eating the macaroni out of the pot (he let him pour in the orange cheese powder) and afterward they fenced with the marshmallow sticks and waved the torches they made against the darkness and when the marshmallows were black and sagging, pulled out their uncooked hearts and licked their fingers. At some point it started to rain, and standing in the double door of the barn, the boy on a pile of boards, they could see the shapes of the elk coming into the meadow and they watched, staring into the dark, until the only way you could tell the herd was still there was that every few seconds one would shiver the rain out of its hide, making a small white cloud like breath. He could hardly make out the boy next to him: now his hand against the dark wood, now the plane of his cheek. "Dad?" he heard him say. "Do the elk have to sleep in the rain?"

"I think they're used to it," he said.

"You think they're cold?"

"Hard to say. Wet, anyway."

He put his arm around him—that tiny shoulder, tight as a nest—but aware of the weight, didn't let it rest completely. And they were quiet. Thank you, he thought, then mouthed the words to himself in the dark.

The rain made sleep easy. The two of them lay side by side in their softly crackling sleeping bags like pods, identical but for size. When he crawled out of the tent in the middle of the night to pee, the rain had stopped and he could see stars through the missing places in the roof. Later he thought he heard the rain again, but he'd been dreaming something about rain, and with the boy's rib cage under his arm, he slept.

IN THE MORNING the ground was soaked but he managed to get up a fire anyway. There was a heavy mist on the meadow, and it rose and drifted across the sky in long smoky sweeps. He couldn't remember the last time he'd seen something so beautiful. After breakfast they would leave their packs in the barn and explore. He'd promised his mother he'd have him back by ten. They didn't have to leave till noon.

The morning went too quickly, but he didn't mind. Better not to overdo it the first time. There would be other trips. He wanted to leave things undone. They walked a mile up the trail to a tributary of the river, where they found a big track pressed into the mud that looked like it might have been a cat's, and then it was time to go.

They were about a mile from the river when he realized that coming back he'd have to hold the stick in his left hand: The current would be coming from the other side now. It didn't matter;

his right shoulder was a little stiffer, so sitting the boy on his arm would be a little less comfortable, but that was all. It shouldn't matter much.

He had thought the river sounded louder before they came out of the woods, and it did. There was no mistake—it had grown stronger overnight. He understood right away. It wasn't the rain—there hadn't been enough to make a difference. It was the afternoon melt: In the mountains, forty miles away, the snowfields were melting in the sun. They'd slow in the evening cold, and not pick up again until the following afternoon. He knew this. He'd forgotten.

Still, it didn't amount to all that much. Looking at the river, you could hardly tell the difference. The boy had run on ahead; he could see him throwing sticks into the current. He'd just have to take it slow, that's all. Anyway, it wasn't as though they could wait till the next morning; he'd promised he'd have him back. There was no way of letting her know. But it didn't matter. Slow down, fella, he said to himself, but the sound of his own voice made him uncomfortable, so he didn't say anything more.

He walked in over the wet stones and splashed some water on his face, then pointed out where the current ran clear and flat over fist-sized rocks, thigh-deep. He was thinking too much. He took off his shoes and socks and pants, re-tied his shoes, and slipped on the two packs, the belt dangling free.

"OK, kiddo," he said, "same thing as yesterday. You just stay put right here, and I'll wave from the other side."

The current was stronger—he could tell right away from the pull on his calves, the sound it made—not much stronger, but stronger. He worked slowly, picking his path, lifting the stick completely clear of the water and jabbing it down, leaning into the current, avoiding any rocks larger than a plate. It was a good track. With a river of any size, there was only one way—straight across, slightly quartering upstream. You had to pick your path and go. You had to plan ahead, never take a step you couldn't move from.

Halfway across he stopped and rested his arm. It felt strange to be standing there, the current wrapping itself hard around his thigh. He looked at his watch. It was taking a little longer. So what? He'd crossed this thing a dozen times. More. Eight years was nothing. Same man, same river.

When he made it to the beach he dumped the packs and waved quickly and started back across. It had gone well. Well enough. His left arm was a little tired but he could rest it on the way back—the current was from the other direction now—and not having the packs made a difference. He tried not to look at the boy sitting where he'd left him on the opposite shore because there was something about him in his blue shorts against the bank of stones he didn't like and because he wanted to keep his eyes on the water, and yet when he slipped, the toe of his right boot catching on the edge of something then sliding over rock as slick as any ice, he was looking straight down into the water. He floundered awkwardly, stumbled, thrust the stick with both hands into the current as if lunging at something under the water, and felt it catch. He hadn't seen it—whatever it was. He breathed, feeling his heart thrashing in his ribs. You never see it, he thought.

There was no point in waiting, so less than a minute after he'd slopped out onto the rocks and flexed his arms like Mr. Universe ("You ready, kiddo?") he squatted down and the boy crawled onto his back. "You see how I almost fell back there?" he said. "You have to be careful. I got a little sloppy."

"I saw an eagle," the boy said. "It was enormous, and it flew right over the river."

"Really?" he said.

THE BOY FELT a little heavier than he had before, and thirty feet in he hoisted him up and shifted the weight. "OK?" he said. He continued on, feeling for edges, probing ahead like a snail testing the air, then stopped and readjusted him again. When he stopped the third time, he knew it was going to be a push. He should have brought the boy across first. He wished he could switch him to his left, hold the stick with his right. He had to stretch his arm for a second, he said. He dropped his arm and the boy dangled from his neck, and then he caught him up and the pressure eased from his windpipe and they continued on. He tried not to look downstream. No point. "How you doin' back there?" he said. He was strong. He could do this.

They didn't go down when it happened, but they should have. How he managed to arrest them in that current, already sliding four, five feet downstream, slipping on one algae-slick rock, then another, he didn't know. How he managed not to turn upstream or down, which would have finished things, he didn't know either. All he knew was that they were still up and the boy was still on his back and he was straightening up, still facing the shore, no more than a broomstick's length from where they'd been a moment earlier. The current was mid-thigh and strong.

He could hear himself, breathing hard. "I'm OK, kiddo. I'm OK. That wasn't good, but we're fine."

They weren't fine. Ignoring the quivering in his shoulder he tried to take stock. The rocks were bigger here. He couldn't get back to where they'd been. He couldn't quarter upstream and intercept the path because there was a flat pale rock the size of a small table in the way, and the water below it was too deep. "Do me a favor, kid," he said. "See if you can feel where my eyes are. That's it, don't worry—I've got you. Now when I count to three, I'll close my left eye and you wipe the sweat out with your thumb, OK?" He could feel the boy's thumb slide gently over his lid.

"Good, now do it again."

There had to be a way—something he couldn't see. There was nothing. A step behind him, the rocks were smaller. It didn't matter. He couldn't step back. Crossing a river meant moving forward, holding the weight on the back leg while the front foot felt for purchase. Turning around was impossible. At some point he'd have to take the full weight of the current with his legs perpendicular to the shore like a tennis player anticipating a serve; unbraced, he'd come off the bottom like nothing at all. A thin stream of panic started in his head, dulling the sound of water; he looked around stupidly, blinking back the sweat. The shore looked like it was behind a screen. He moved his right foot forward, felt it begin to slide, pulled back. Fuck you, he whispered. Fuck you.

They'd get out of this. They had to get out of this. My God, all his other fuck-ups were just preparations for this. This wasn't possible. He could feel the current—strong, insistent, pumping against his thigh like a drunken lover. Was this how it went? One stupid move? One stupid fucking move, and your son on your back? No. He could do this. He tried to remember the strength he'd felt, that rude, beautiful strength, felt it pushing back the curtain of fear. There was nowhere to go.

He could barely bring himself to speak. He couldn't move. The way ahead was impossible. Far below, he could hear the water sucking on the shallow cavity made by his hip. The river. It wanted to be whole, unbroken. It wanted him gone. He could see it, forming and re-forming, thick-walled jade, smoothing out its sides with its thumbs like a hypnotized potter. The water blurred. He wanted to scream for help. There was no one— just the rushing plain of the river, the trees. He couldn't move. A muscle in his shoulder was jerking like a poisoned animal. What combination of things? Everything had come together. He couldn't move. He was barely holding on. There was no way. The river ahead was smooth, deep, gliding over brown boulders trailing beards of moss in the deep wind. He wanted to laugh. For a second, he felt the hot, shameful fire of remorse and then unending pity—for himself, for the boy on his back, for the heartbreak and absurdity of the world as it is, and at that moment he remembered hearing about a fourteenth-century priest who, personally taking the torch from the executioner, went down the line of victims tied to their stakes and kissed each one tenderly on the cheek before lighting the tinder.

"Dad, you OK?" he heard his son saying as if from some other place. There was nowhere to go. It didn't matter. They had to go.

And then he heard his own voice, answering. "I'm OK, buddy," it said. "You just hang on."

Acknowledgments

I OWE A DEBT OF GRATITUDE TO MY FORMER EDITOR at *Harper's*, Ben Metcalf, for his superb eye, his conversation, and his uncompromising skill with the knife; to Bill Clegg, my agent at the time many of these stories were written, for his careful, nuanced reading; to Stuart Dybek, Sven Birkerts, Geraldine Brooks, Laura Furman, Ann Patchett, and Nick Flynn for giving a number of these tales a shot at the light; and to Jill Bialosky and the folks at Norton for providing them with a good home.

In an equally important way, my heartfelt thanks go out to all those who over the years took the time to say they'd been troubled or touched by something I'd written, among them (the few will have to stand in for the many) Cyd Oppenheimer, Kerry Demers, Raegan Kowalski, Peter Frinton, Vivian Nunez, Monica Richter, Jeff Trenner, Amy Lemmer, Milena Horakova, and Matthew Geyer. Their reminders that an imagined bit of life can resonate in someone else's heart have been a small, sustaining miracle to me, and I'm grateful to them all.